Dear Parent:

Psst . . . you're looking at t[illegible] of Reading. It's called comics.

STEP INTO READING® COMIC READERS are a perfect step in learning to read. They provide visual cues to the meaning of words and helpfully break out short pieces of dialogue into speech balloons.

Here are some terms commonly associated with comics:

PANEL: A section of a comic with a box drawn around it.
CAPTION: Narration that helps set the scene.
SPEECH BALLOON: A bubble containing dialogue.
GUTTER: The space between panels.

SPEECH BALLOON
I'm happy!
PANEL
GUTTER
The next day.
CAPTION

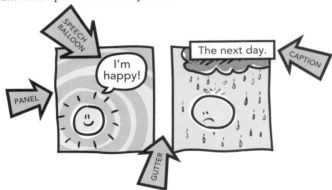

Tips for reading comics with your child:

- **Have your child read the speech balloons while you read the captions.**
- **Ask your child: What is a character feeling? How can you tell?**
- **Have your child draw a comic showing what happens after the book is finished.**

STEP INTO READING® COMIC READERS are designed to engage and to provide an empowering reading experience. They are also fun. The best-kept secret of comics is that they create lifelong readers. **And that will make you the real hero of the story!**

Jennifer L. Holm and Matthew Holm
Co-creators of the Babymouse and Squish series

To Uncle Tim, with love
—T.C.

Copyright © 2024 by Troy Cummings

All rights reserved. Published in the United States by Random House Children's Books, a division of Penguin Random House LLC, New York.

Step into Reading, Random House, and the Random House colophon are registered trademarks of Penguin Random House LLC.

Visit us on the Web!
StepIntoReading.com
rhcbooks.com

Educators and librarians, for a variety of teaching tools, visit us at RHTeachersLibrarians.com

Library of Congress Cataloging-in-Publication Data
Name: Cummings, Troy, author.
Title: Arfy has a ball / by Troy Cummings.
Description: First edition. | New York : Random House Children's Books, 2024. |
Series: Step into reading. | Audience: Ages 4–6. |
Summary: Wanting to play, Arfy searches for the perfect ball.
Identifiers: LCCN 2022060090 (print) | LCCN 2022060091 (ebook) |
ISBN 978-0-593-64373-0 (trade) | ISBN 978-0-593-64374-7 (lib. bdg.) |
ISBN 978-0-593-64375-4 (ebook)
Subjects: CYAC: Dogs—Fiction. | Balls (Sporting goods)—Fiction. | Play—Fiction. |
LCGFT: Animal fiction. | Picture books.
Classification: LCC PZ7.C91494 Arh 2024 (print) | LCC PZ7.C91494 (ebook) | DDC [E]—dc23

Printed in the United States of America
10 9 8 7 6 5 4 3 2 1

First Edition

This book has been officially leveled by using the F&P Text Level Gradient™ Leveling System.

A COMIC READER

STEP INTO READING®

STEP 2

ARFY
HAS A BALL

by Troy Cummings

Random House 🏠 New York

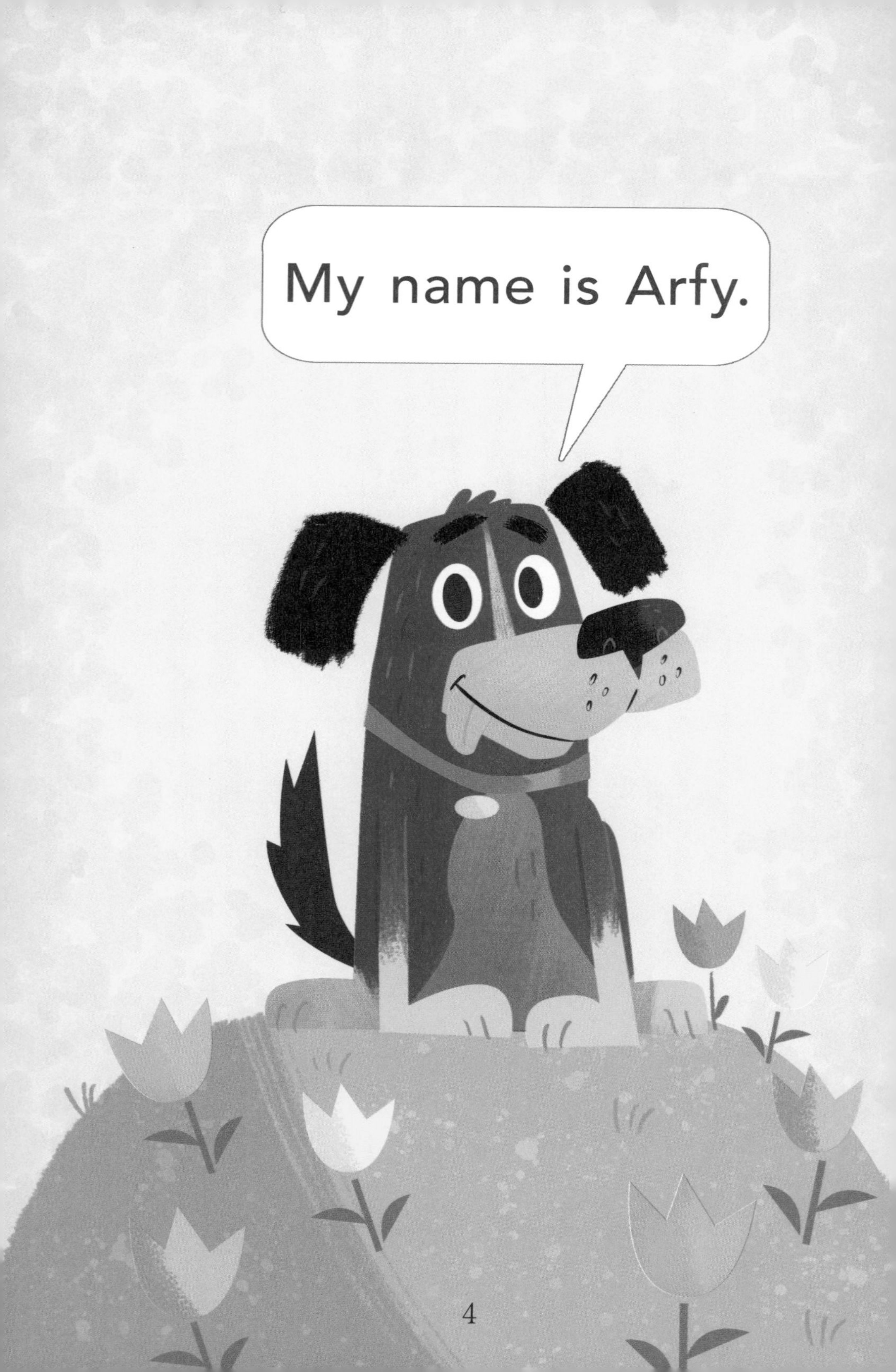
My name is Arfy.

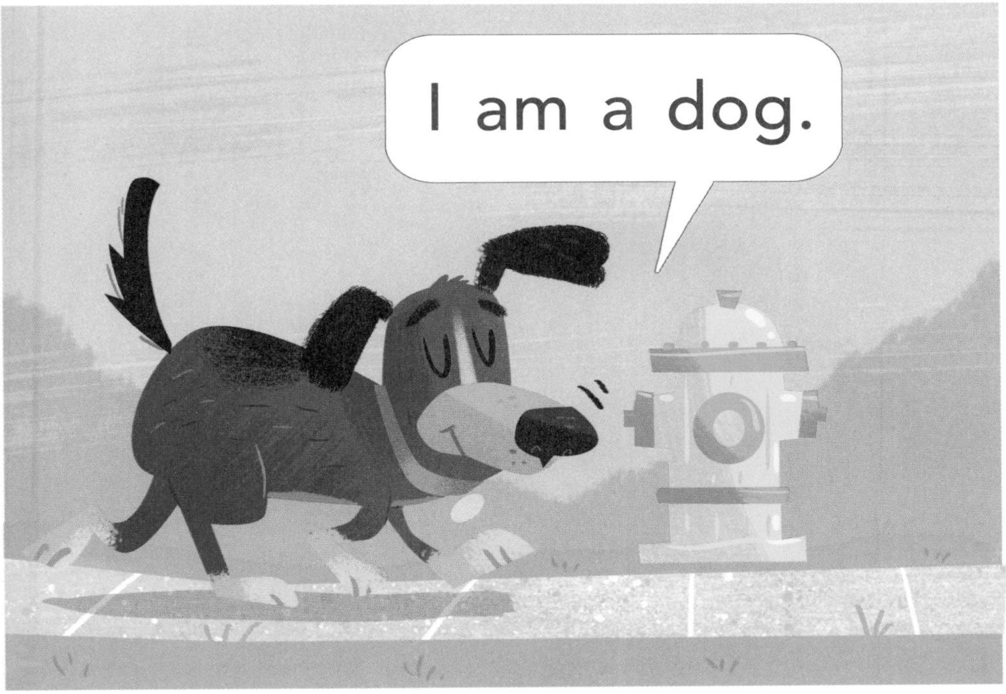
I am a dog.

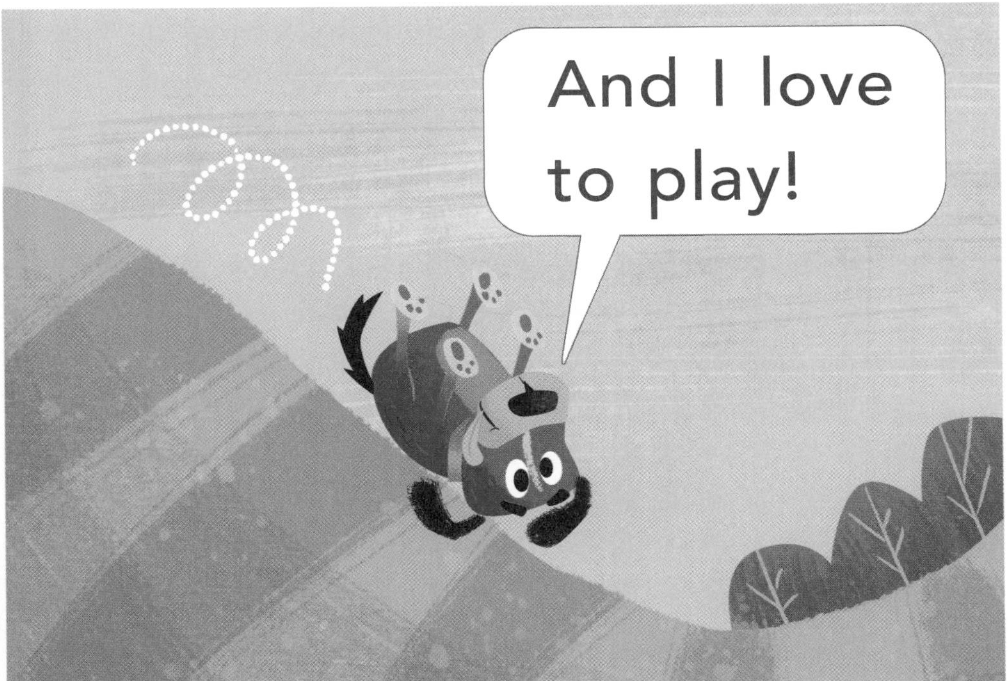
And I love to play!

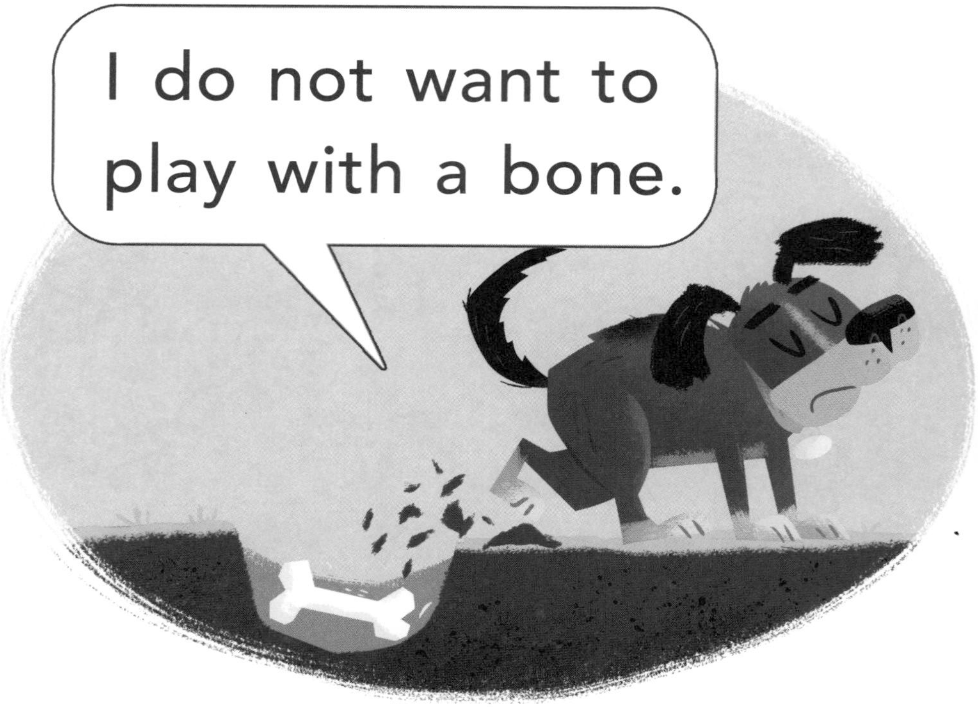
I do not want to play with a bone.

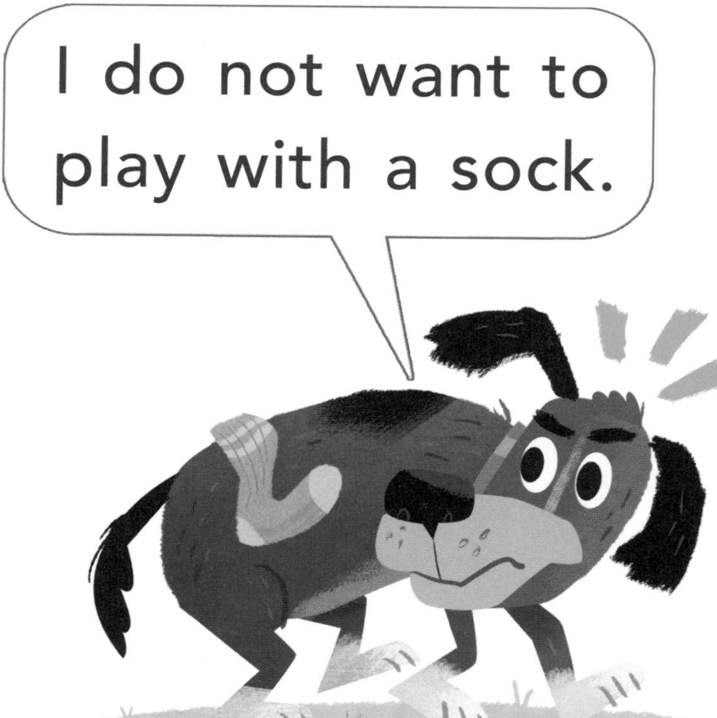
I do not want to play with a sock.

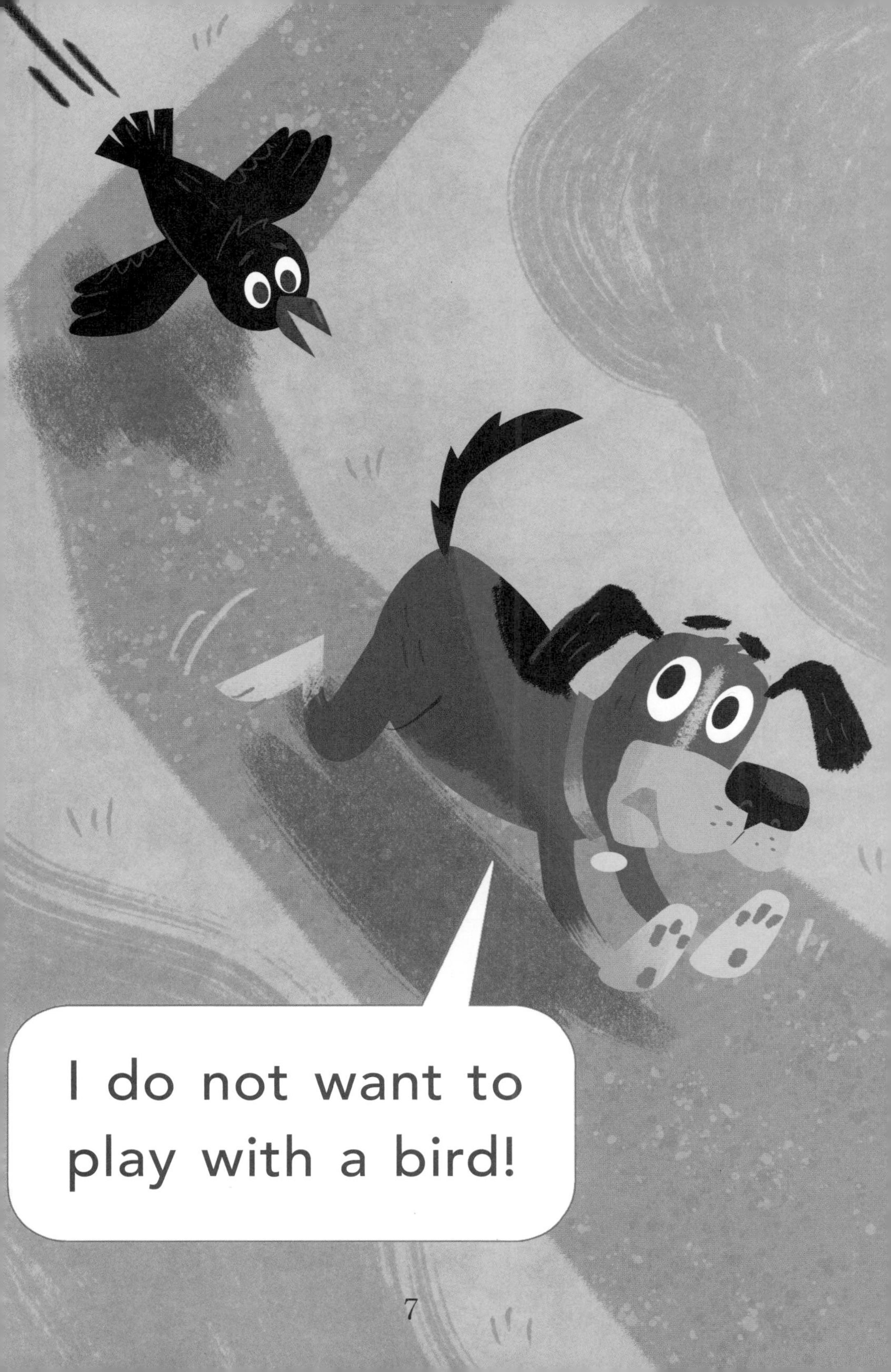
I do not want to play with a bird!

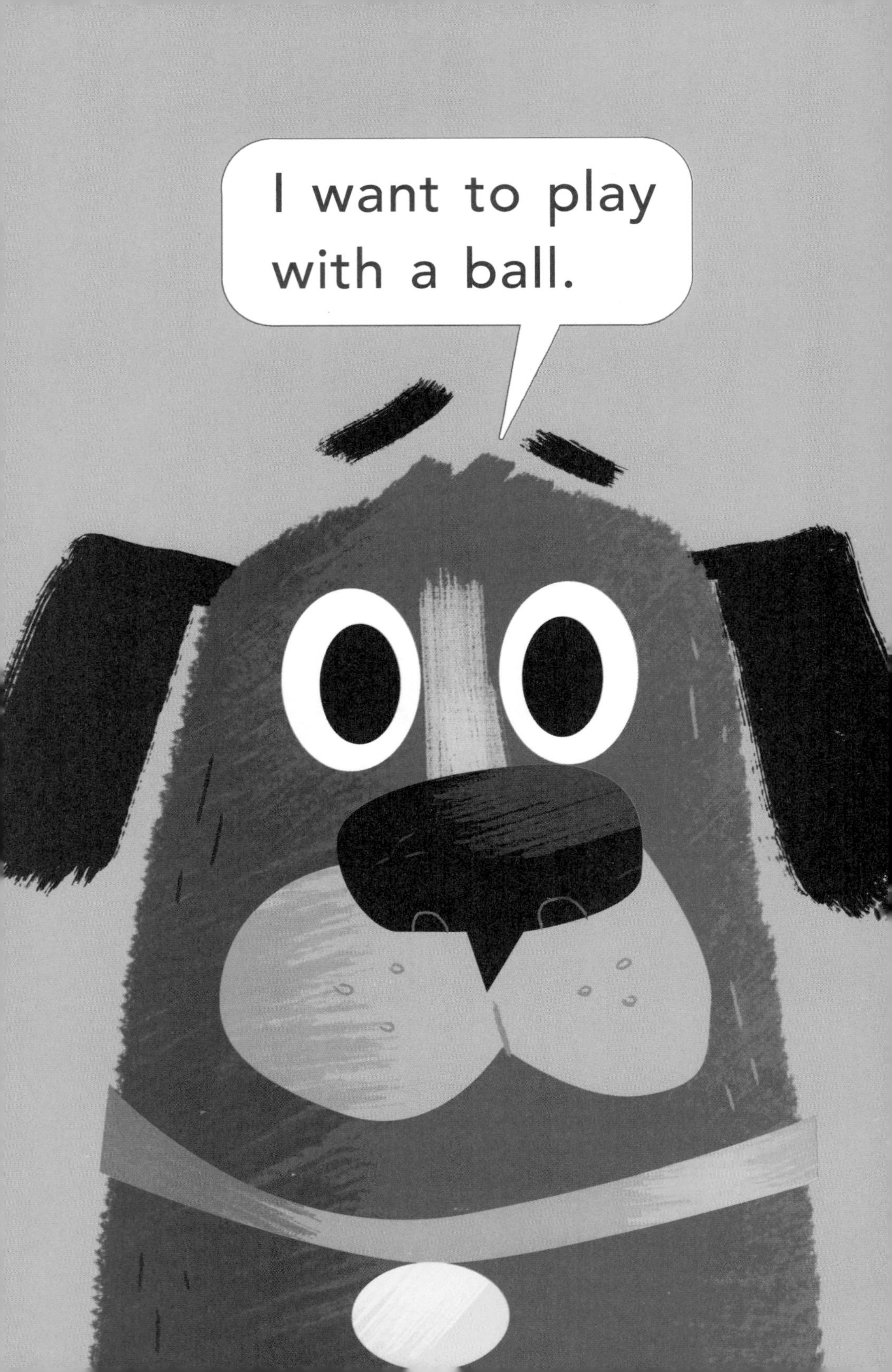
I want to play with a ball.

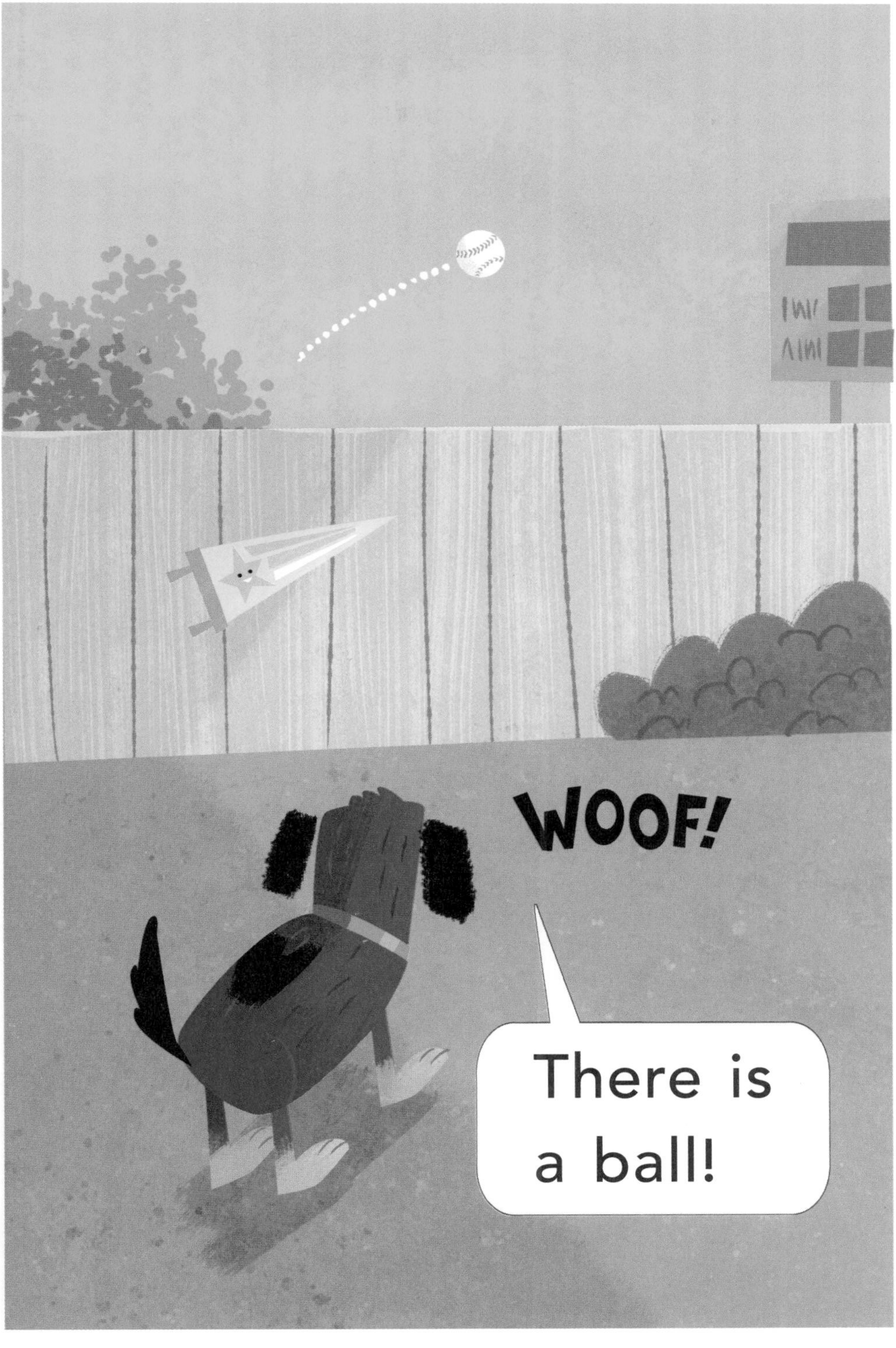
WOOF!
There is a ball!

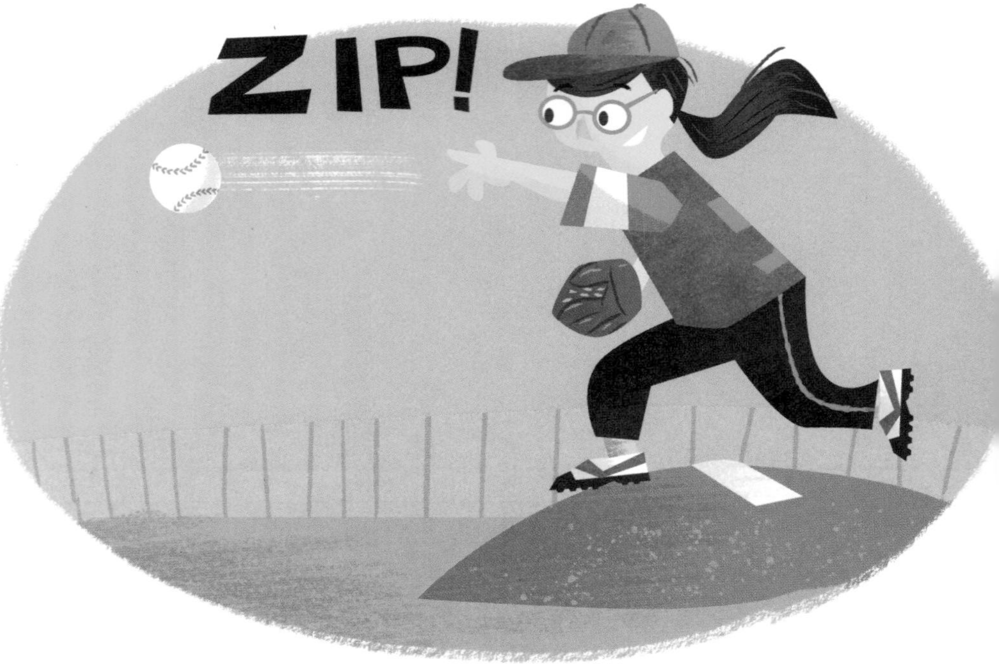
ZIP!

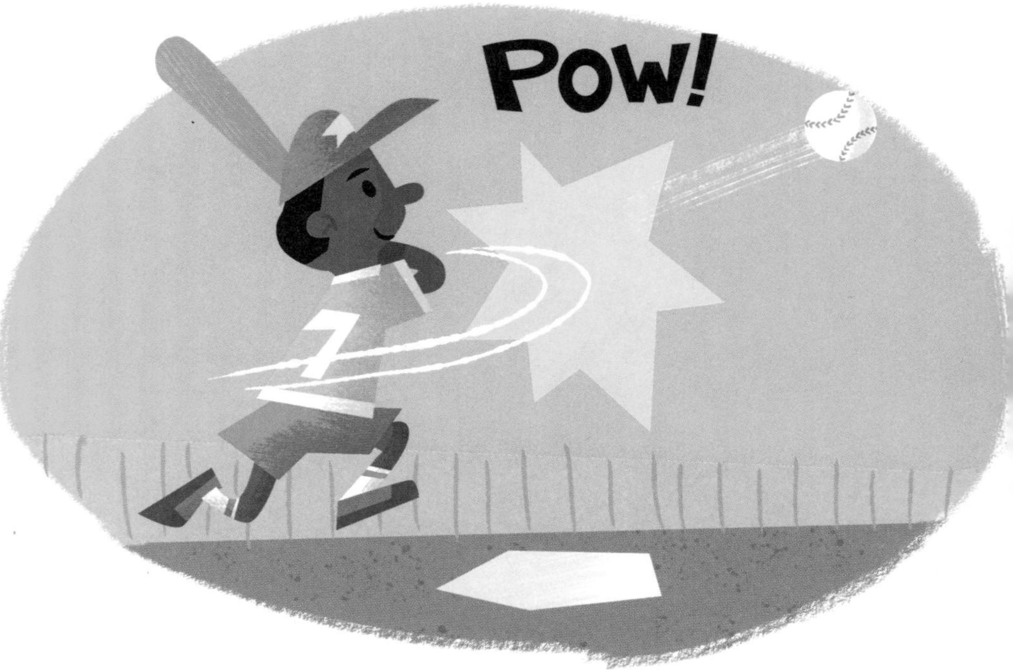
POW!

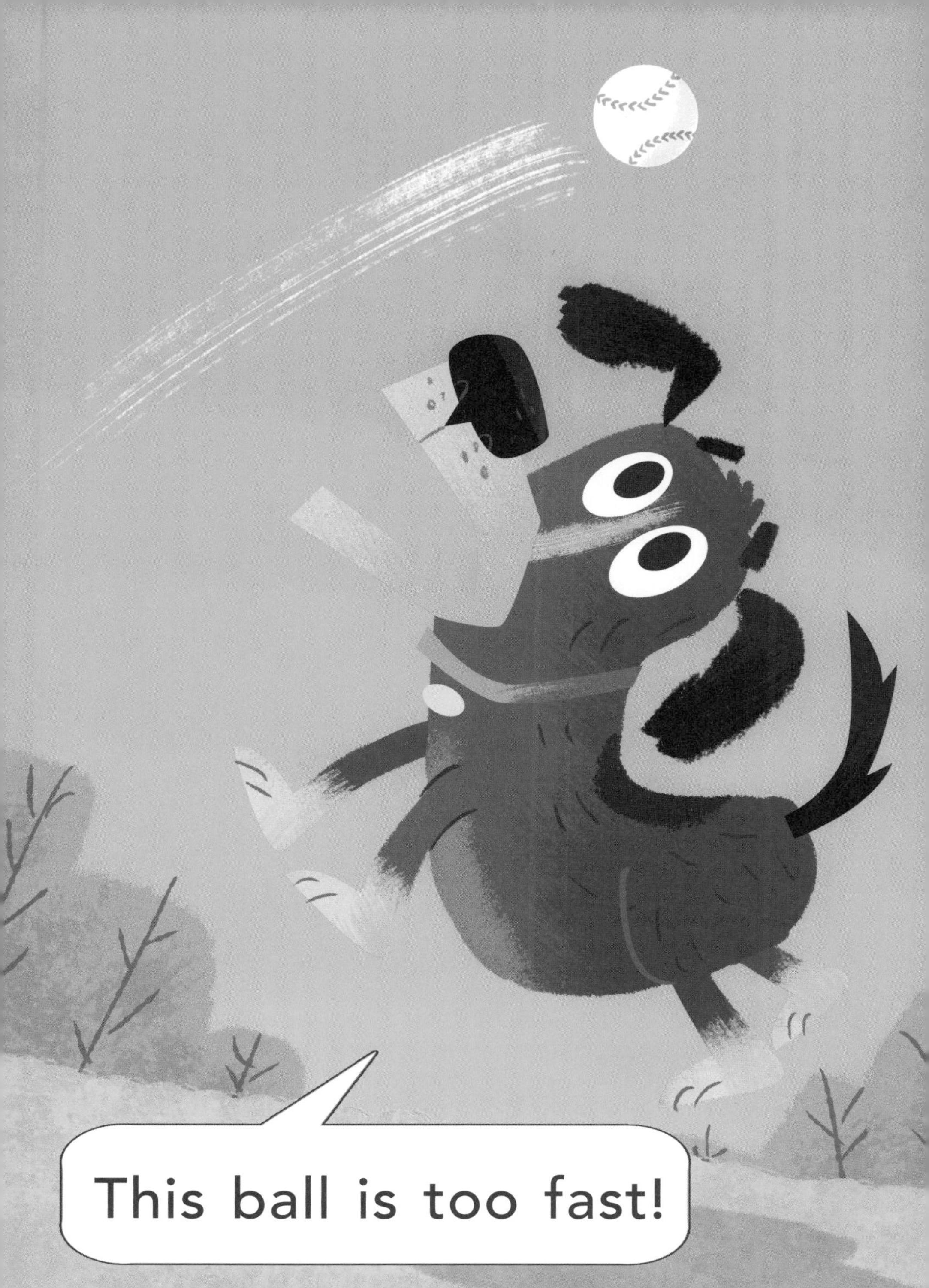
This ball is too fast!

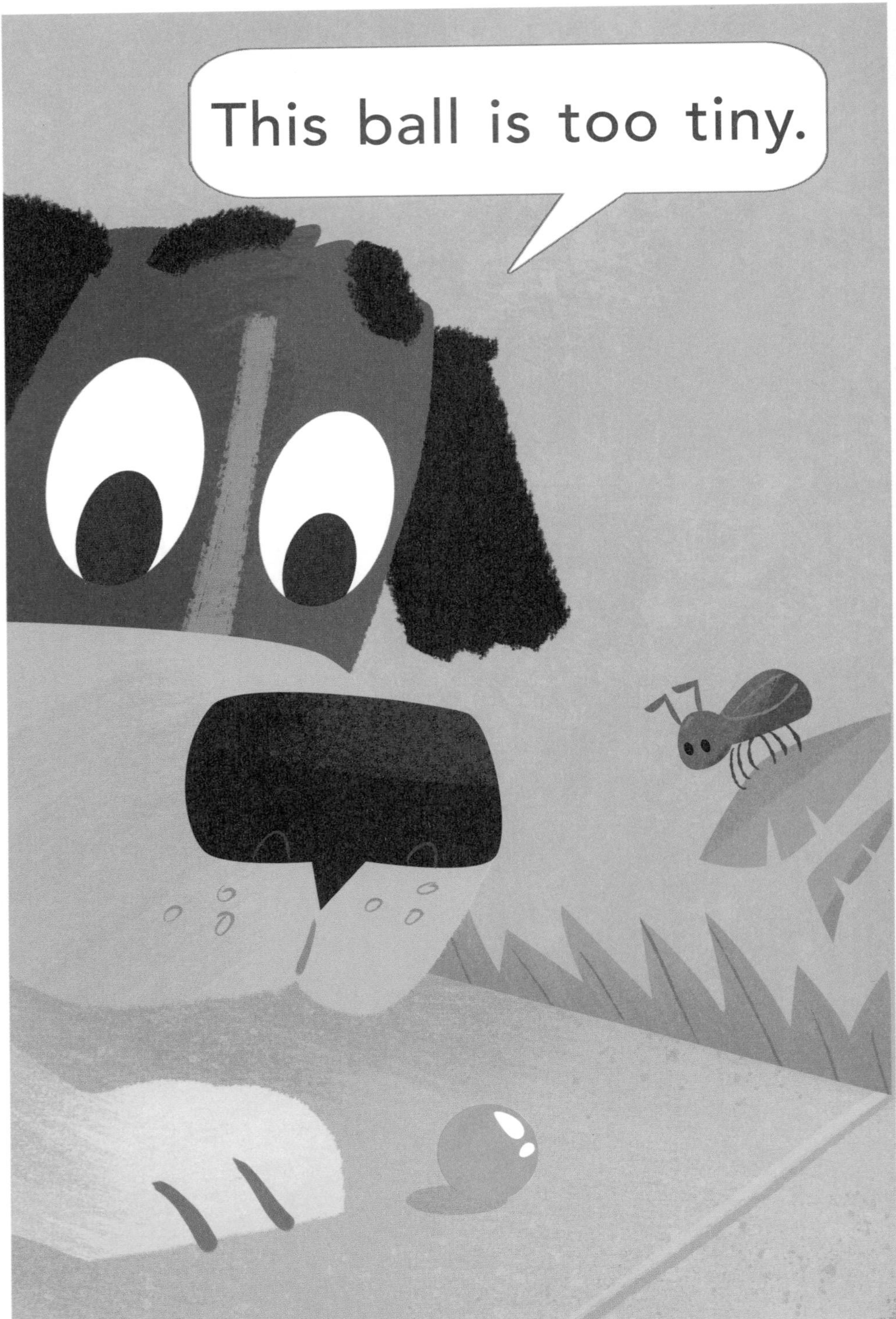
This ball is too tiny.

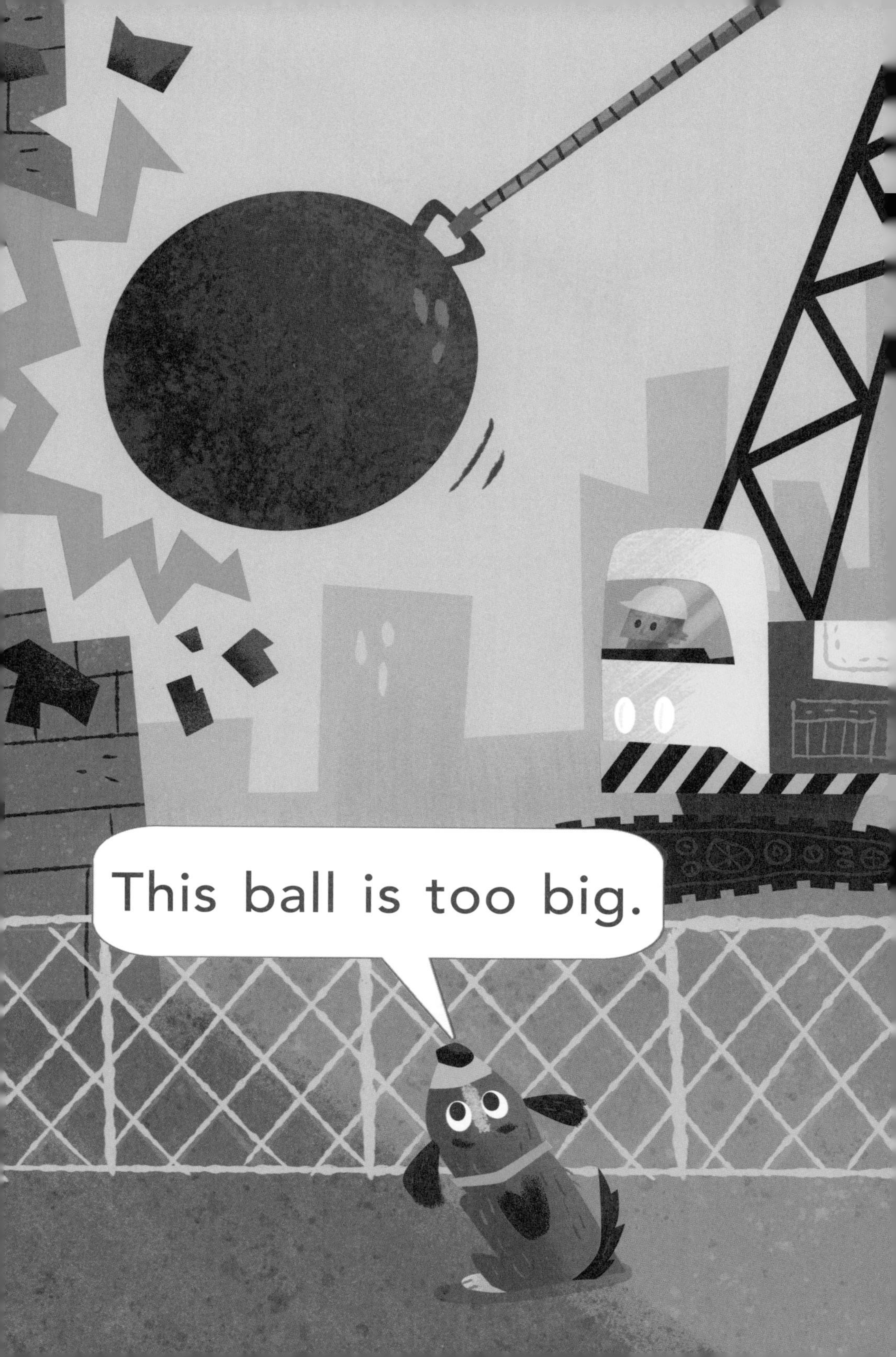
This ball is too big.

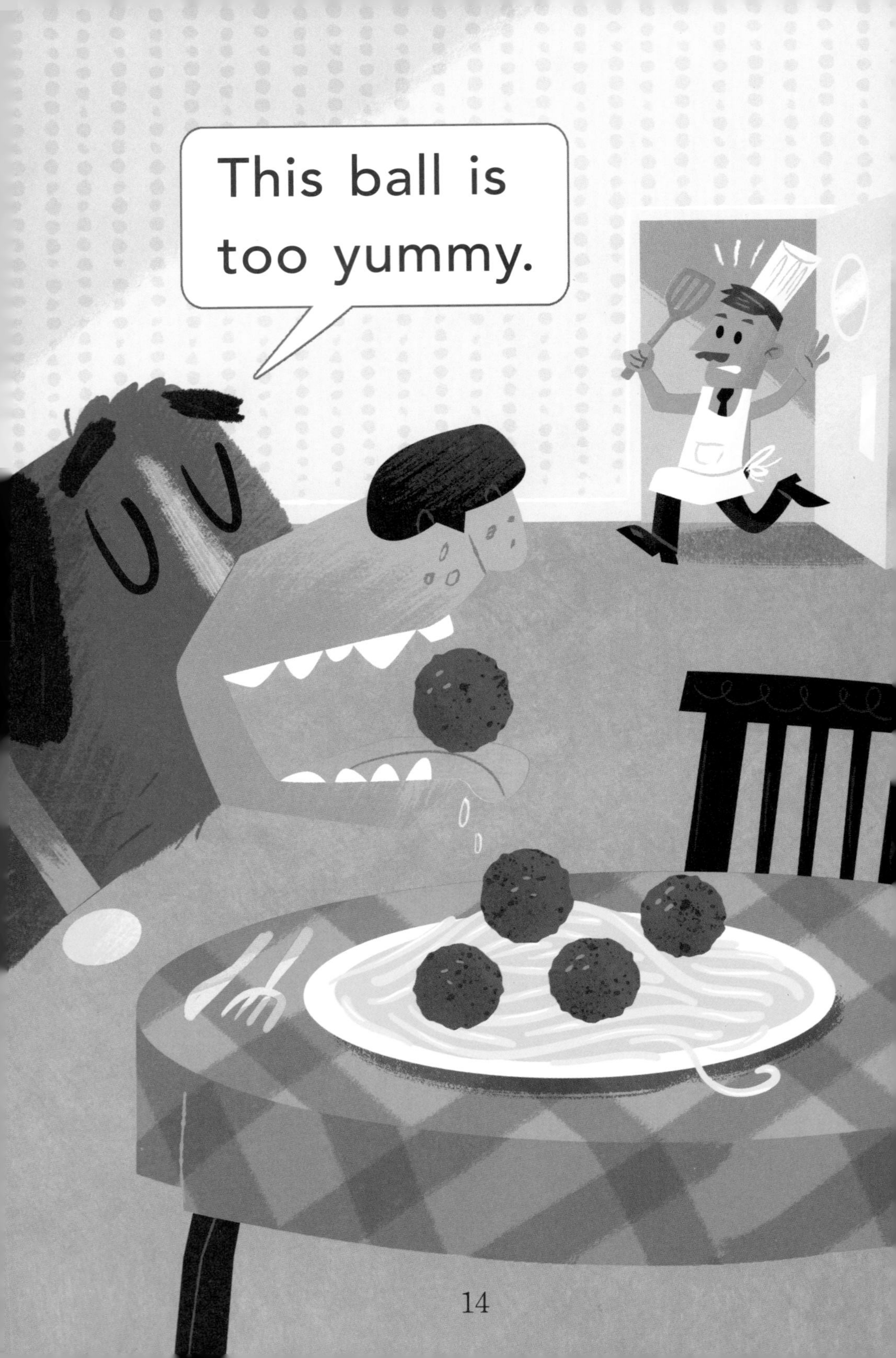
This ball is too yummy.

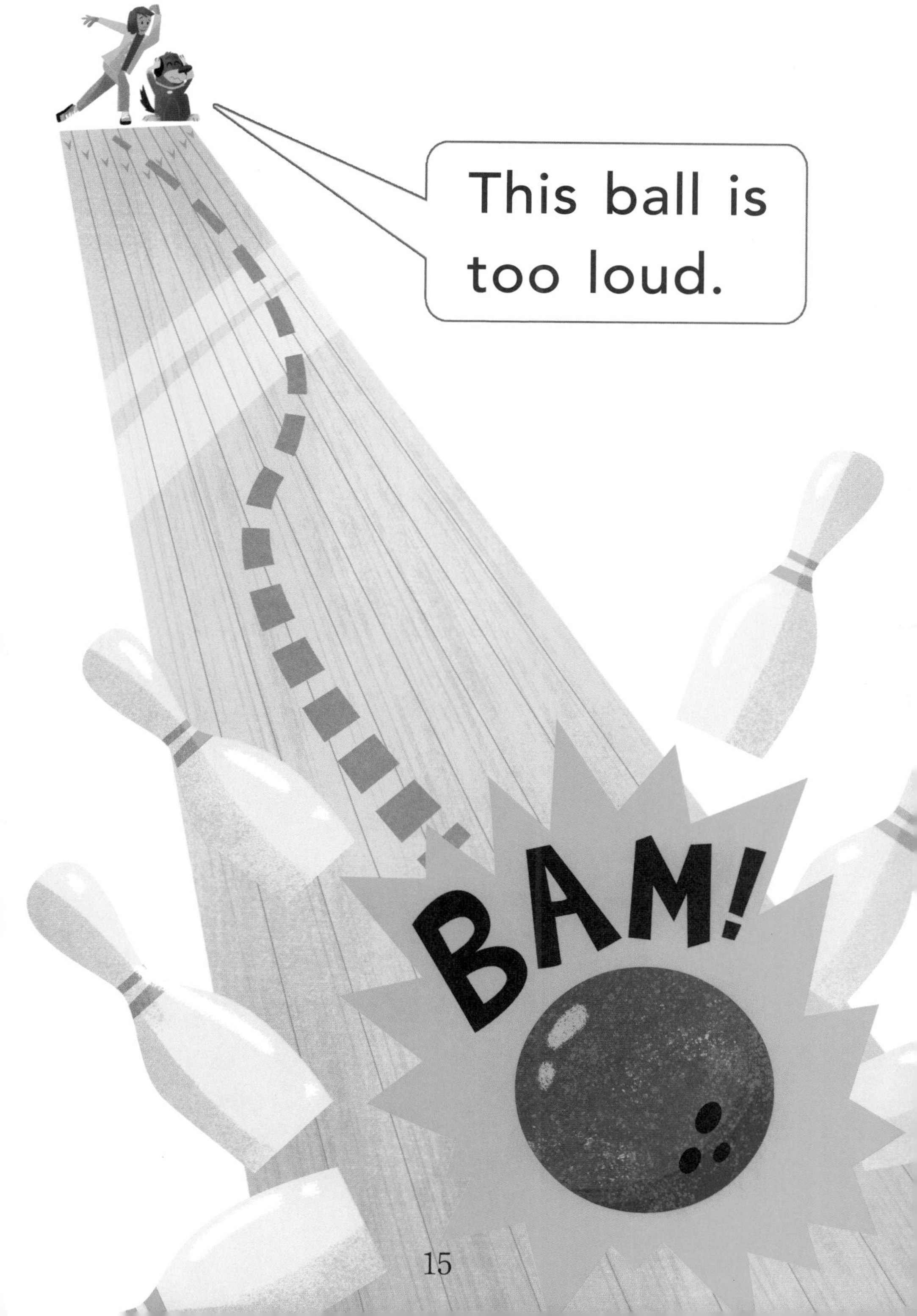
This ball is
too loud.
BAM!

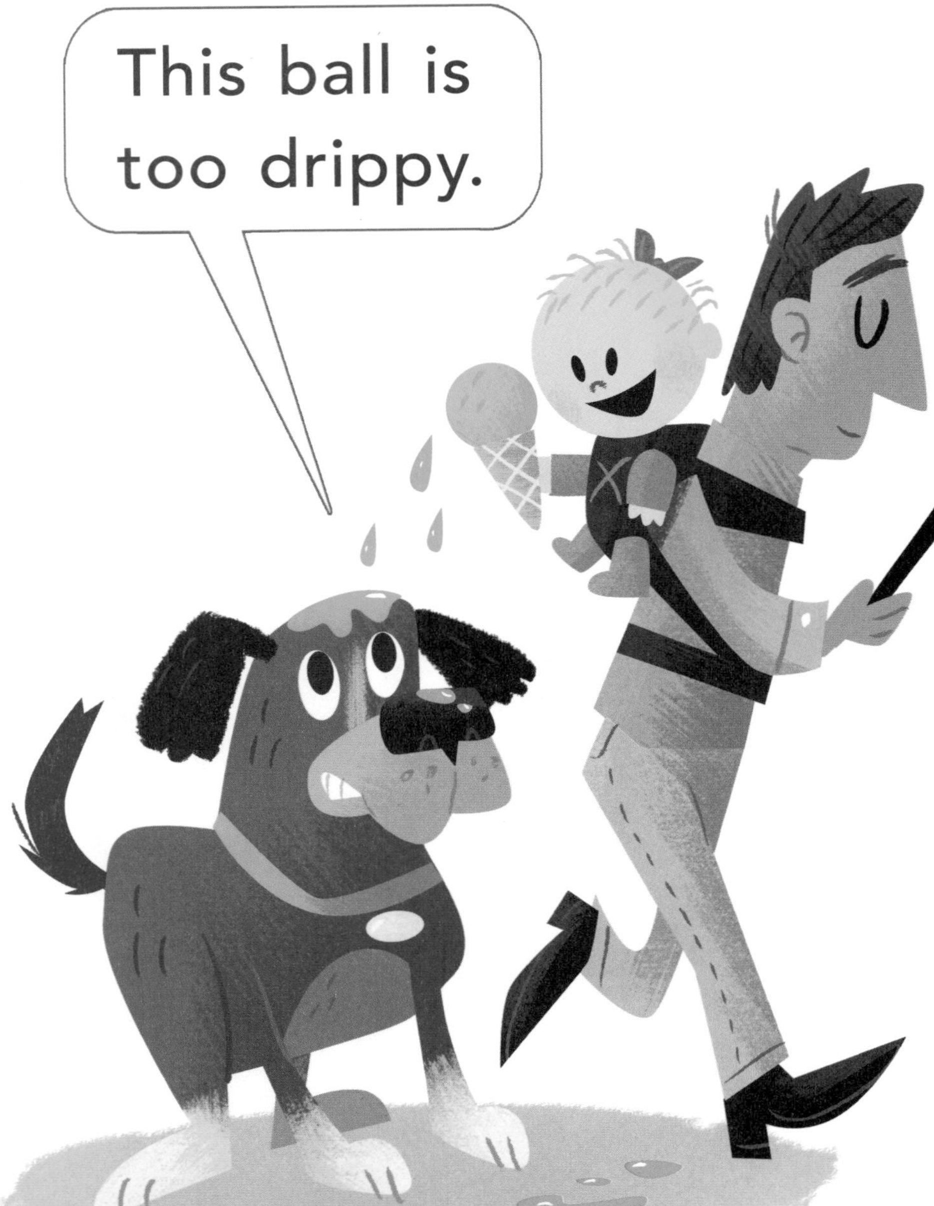
This ball is too drippy.

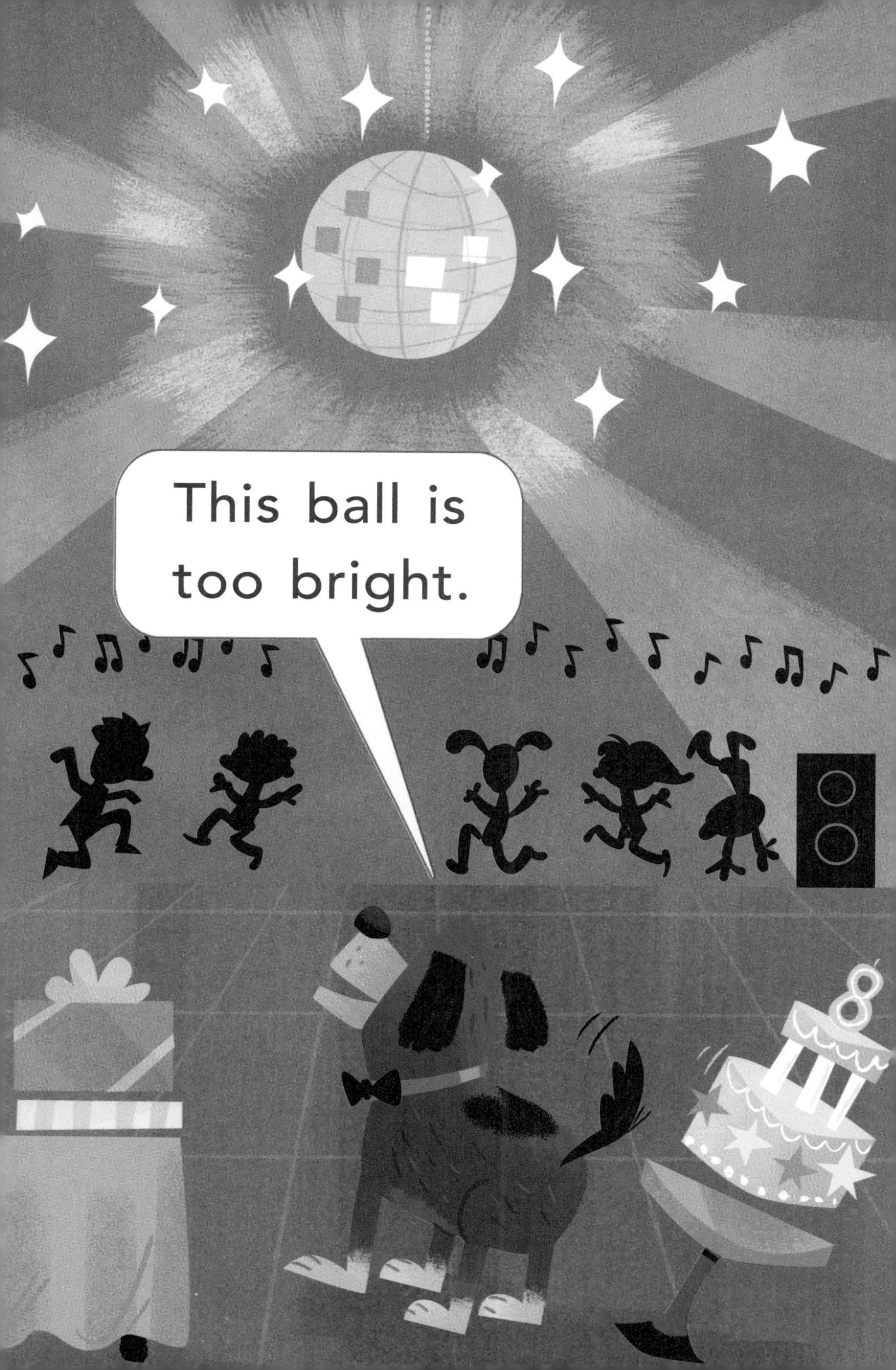
This ball is too bright.

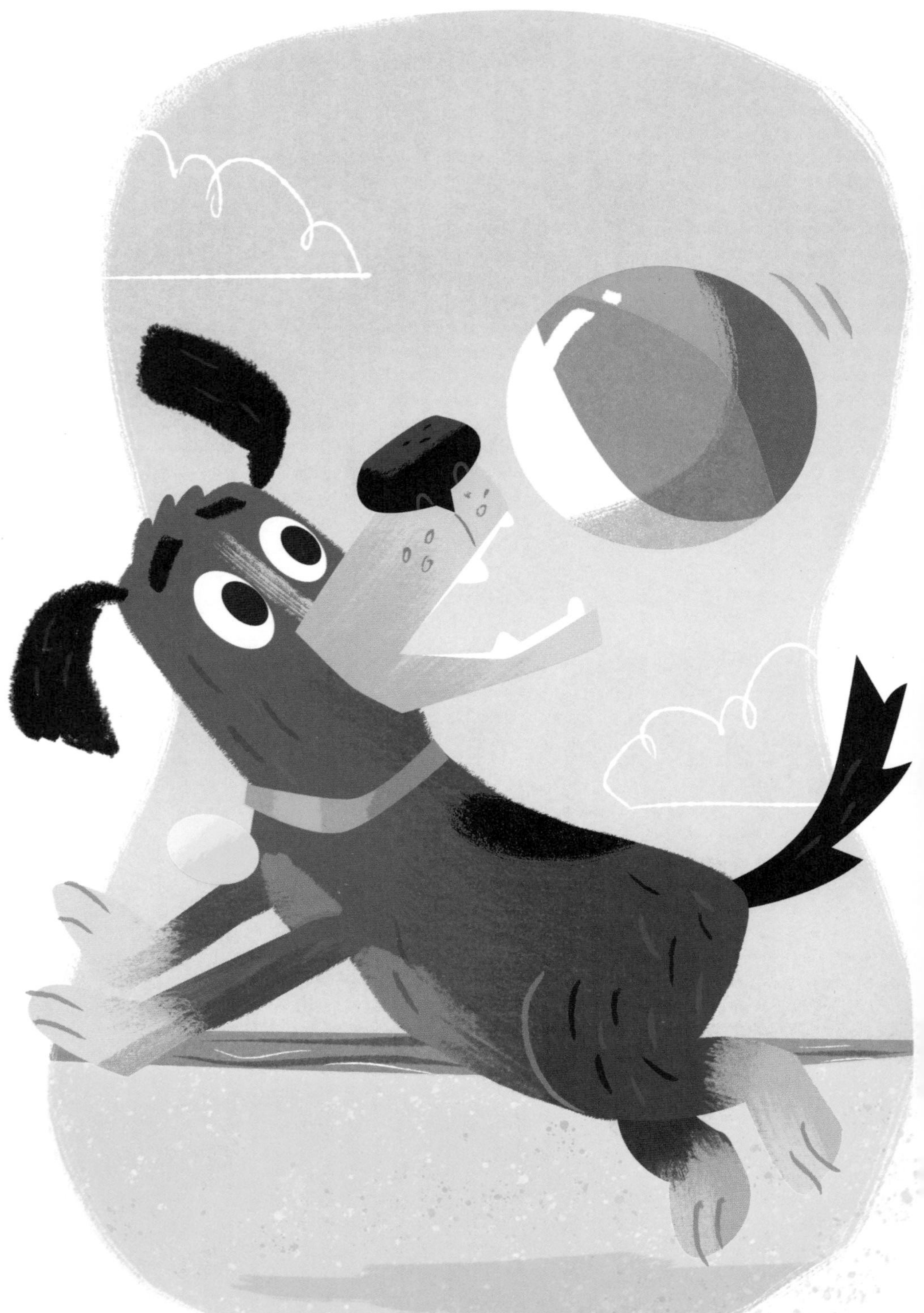

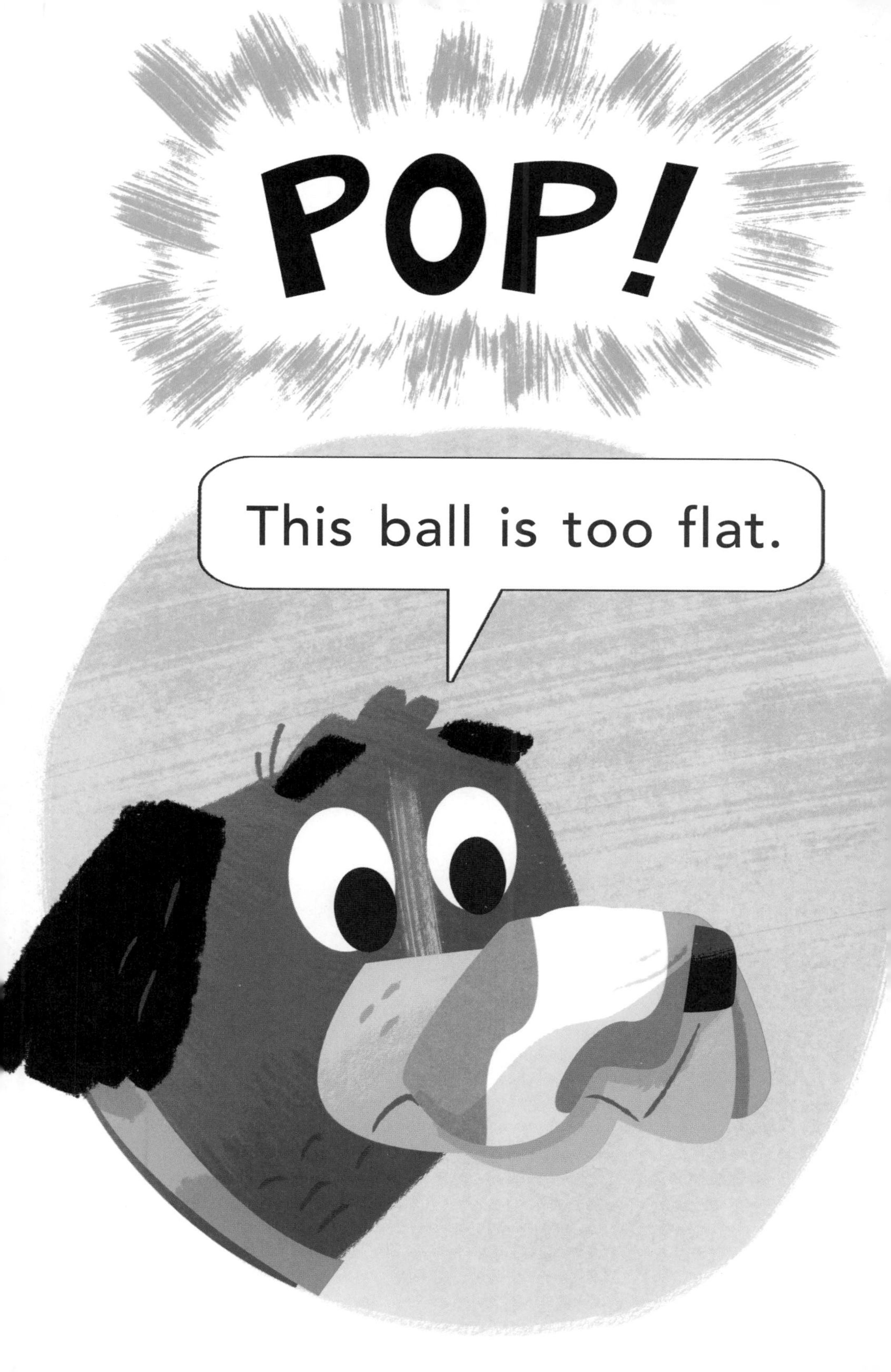
POP!
This ball is too flat.

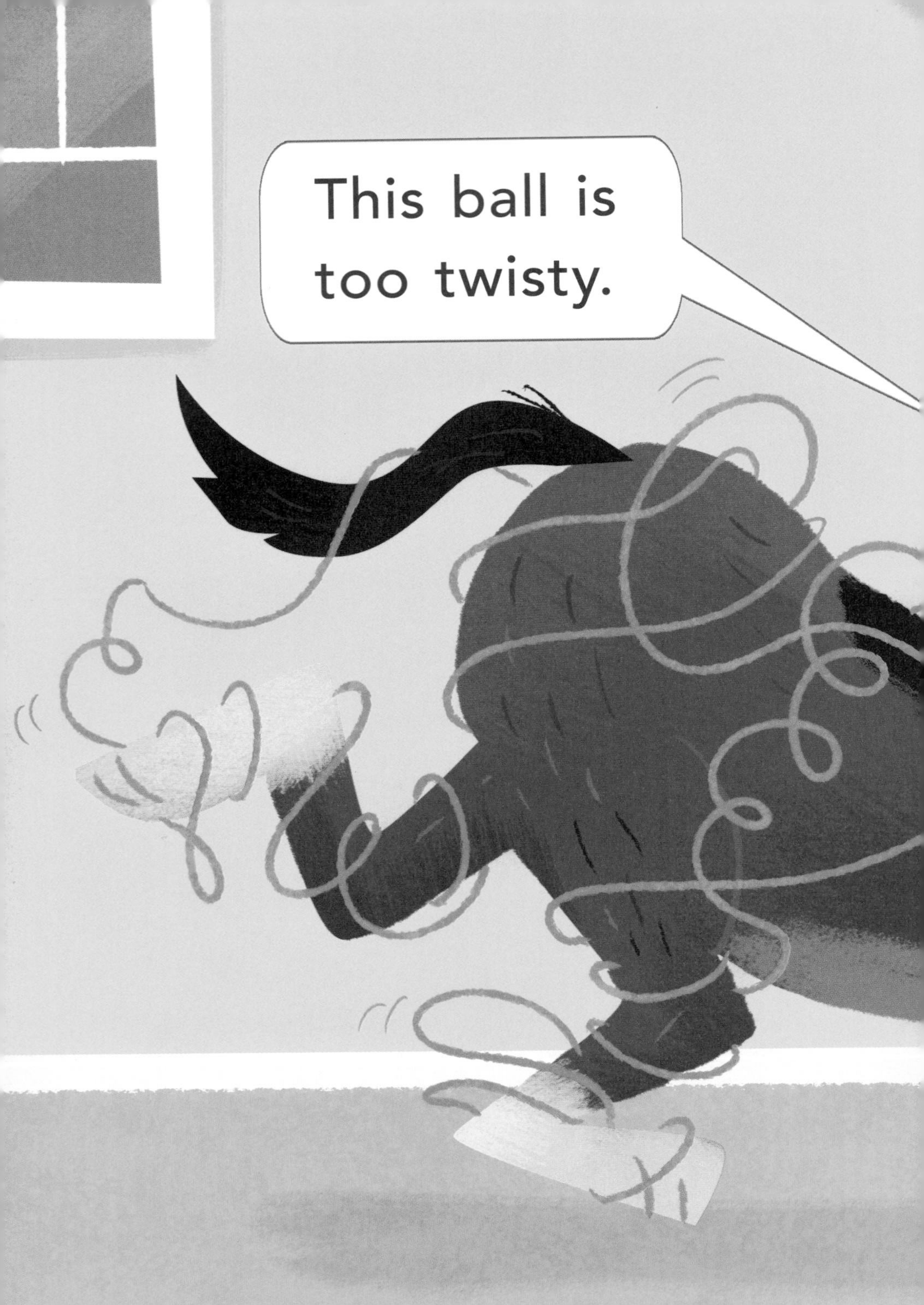
This ball is too twisty.

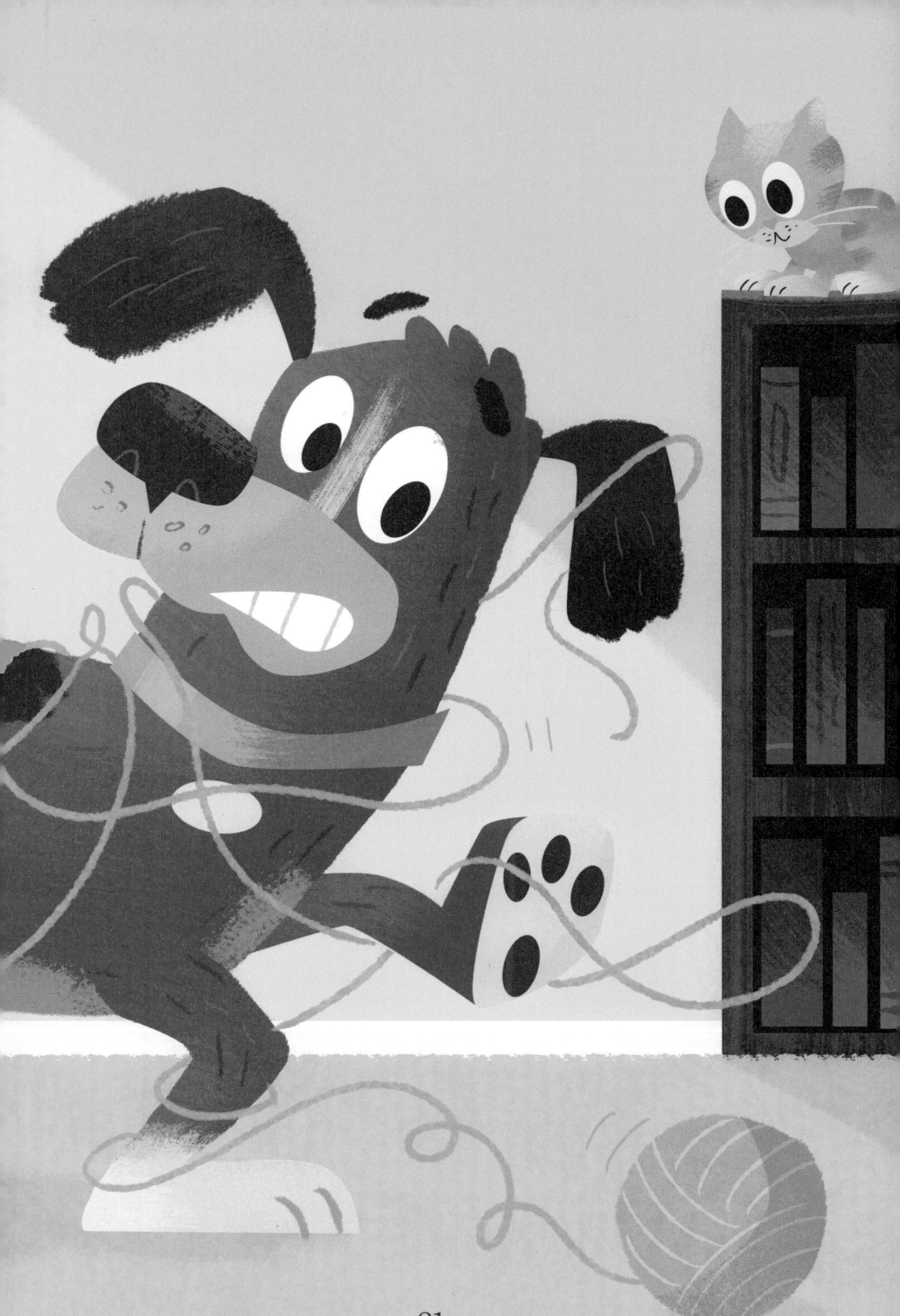

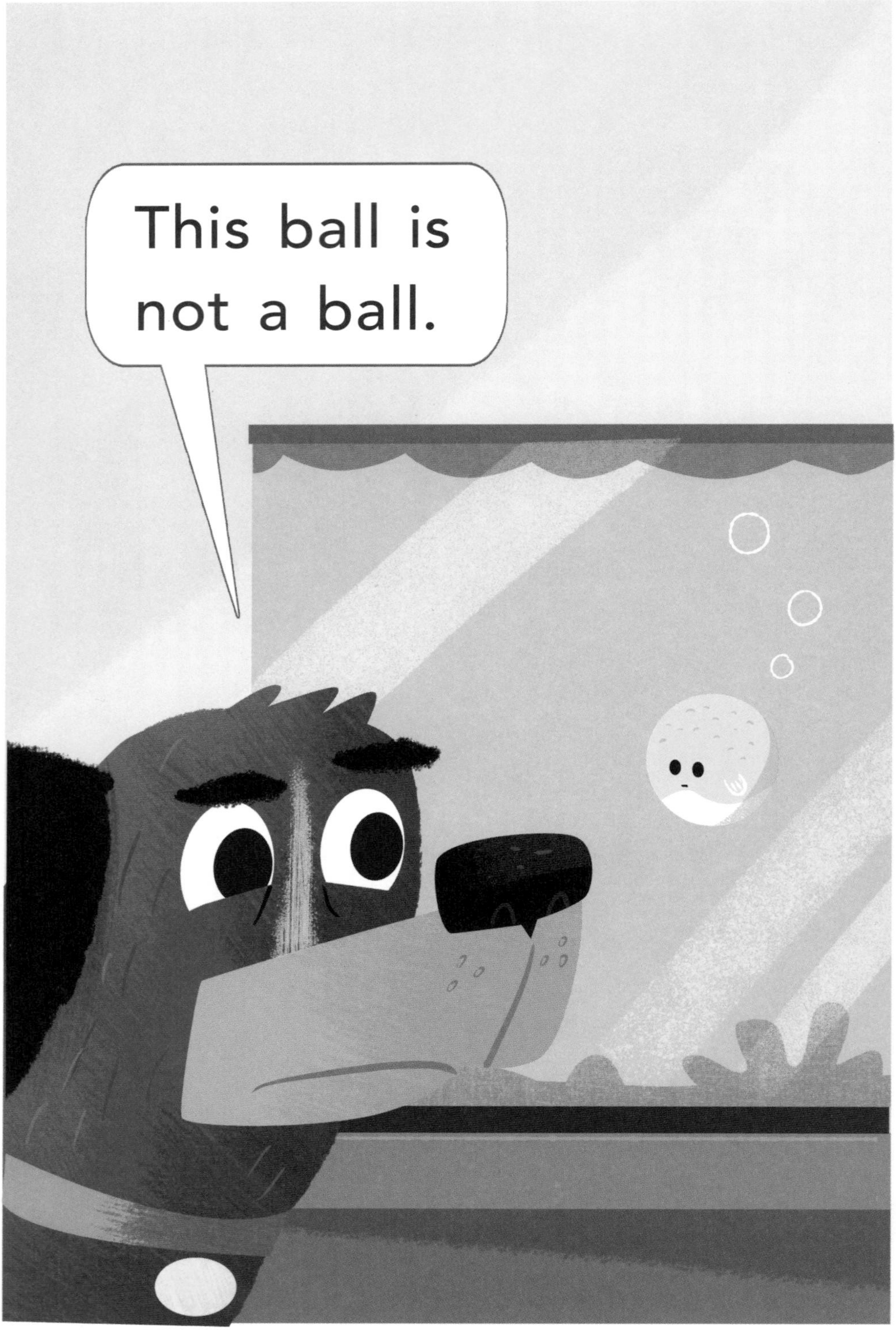
This ball is not a ball.

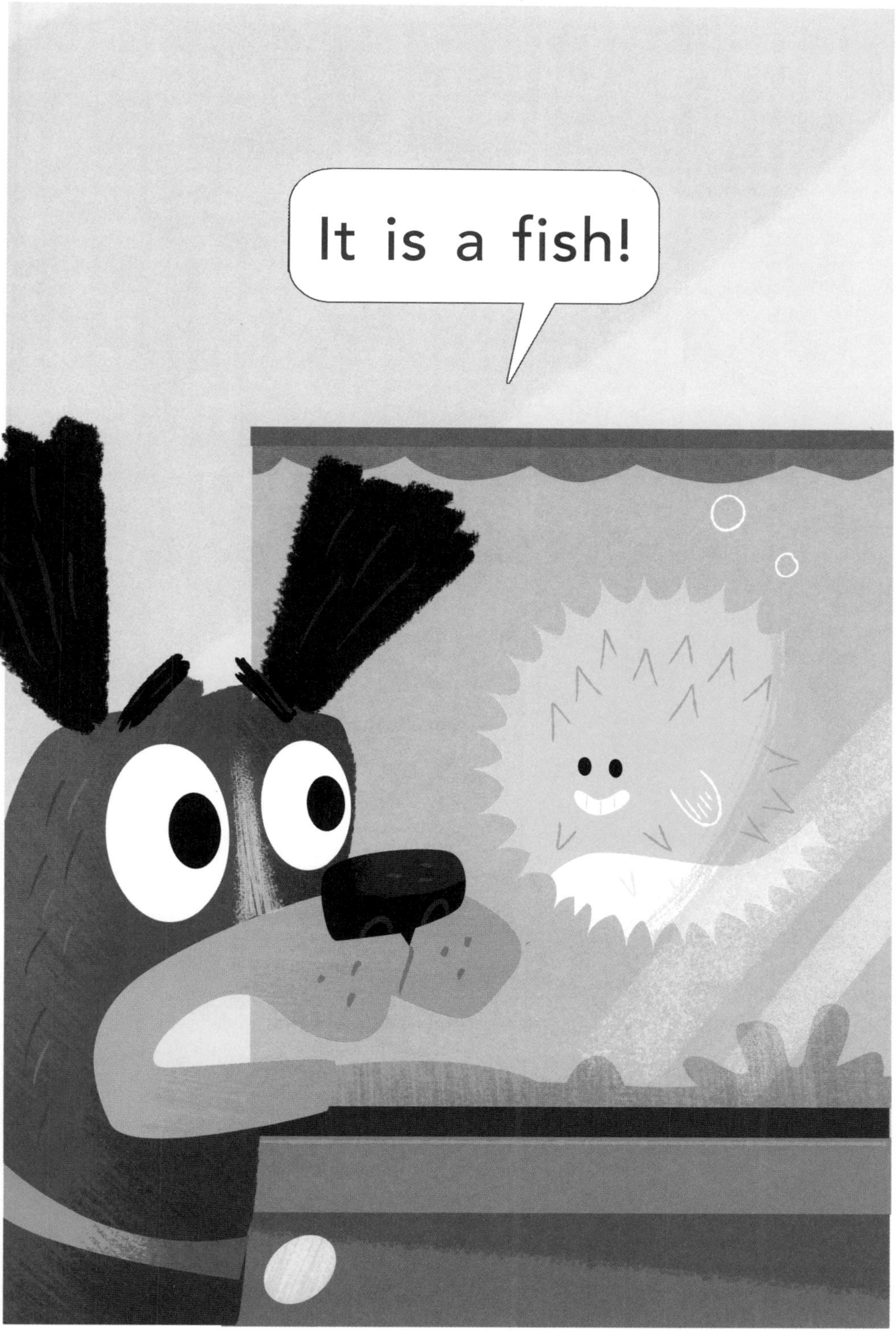
It is a fish!

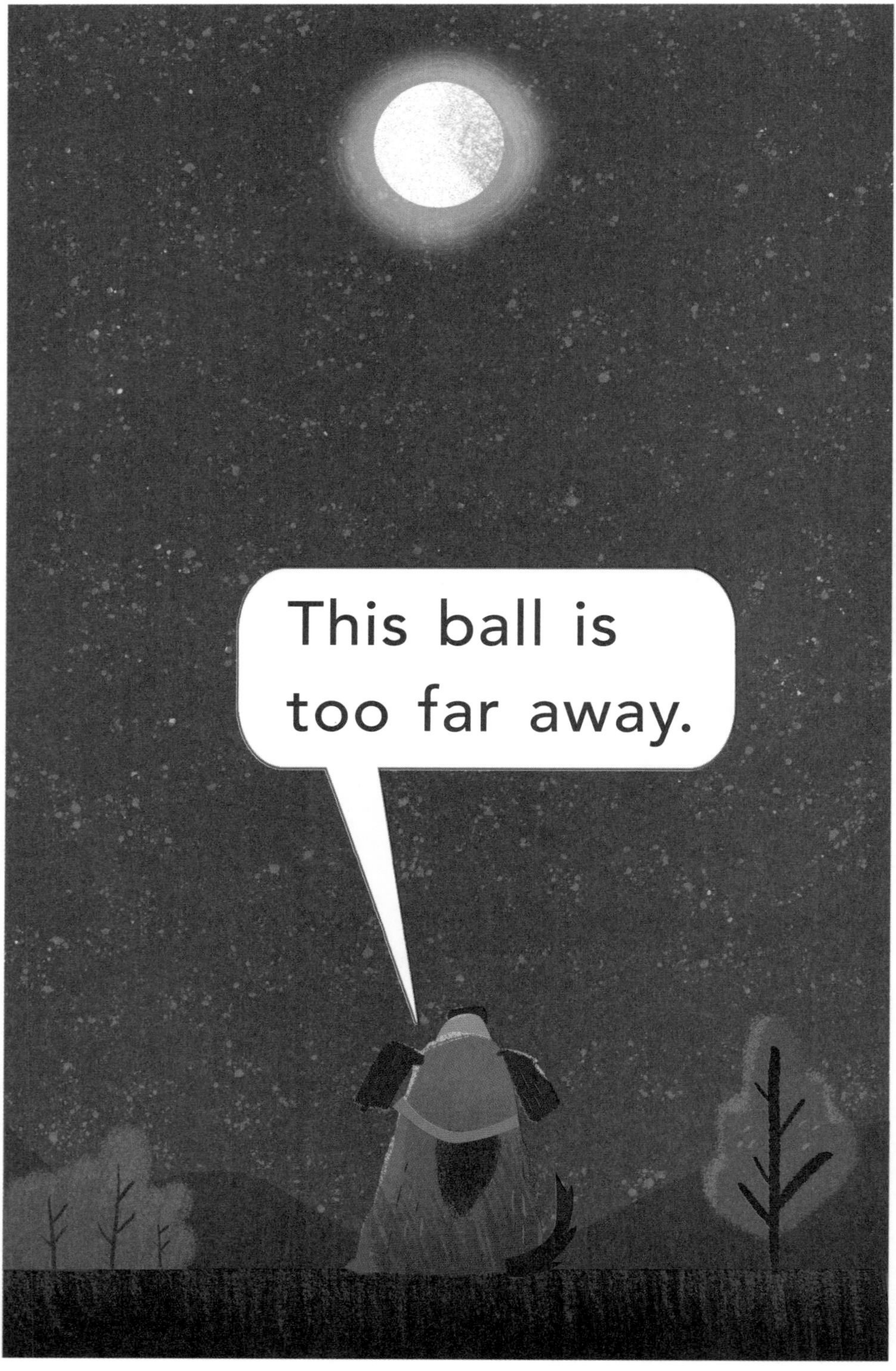
This ball is too far away.

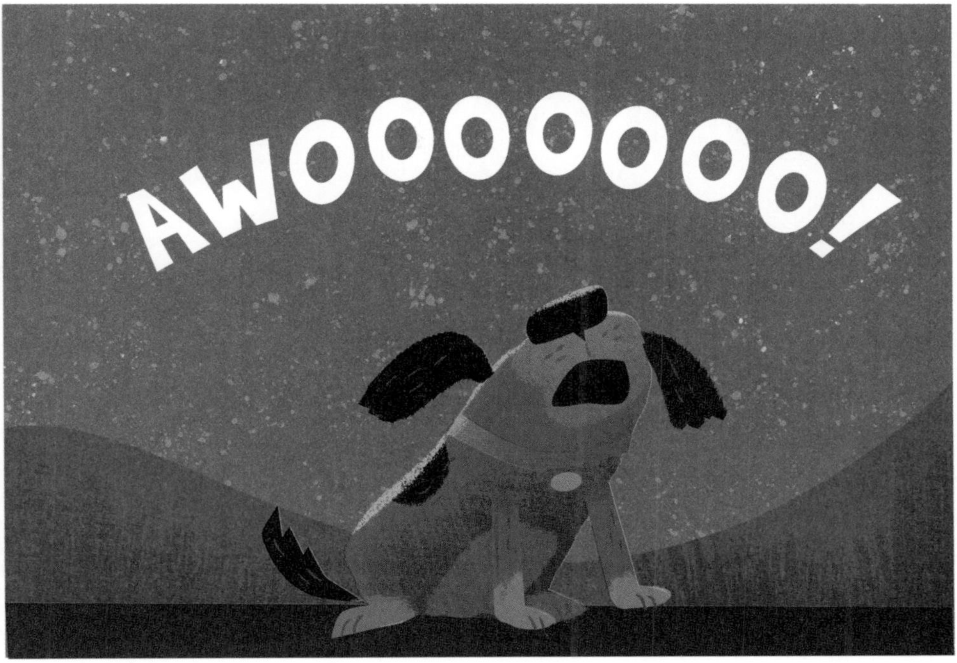
AWOOOOOOO!

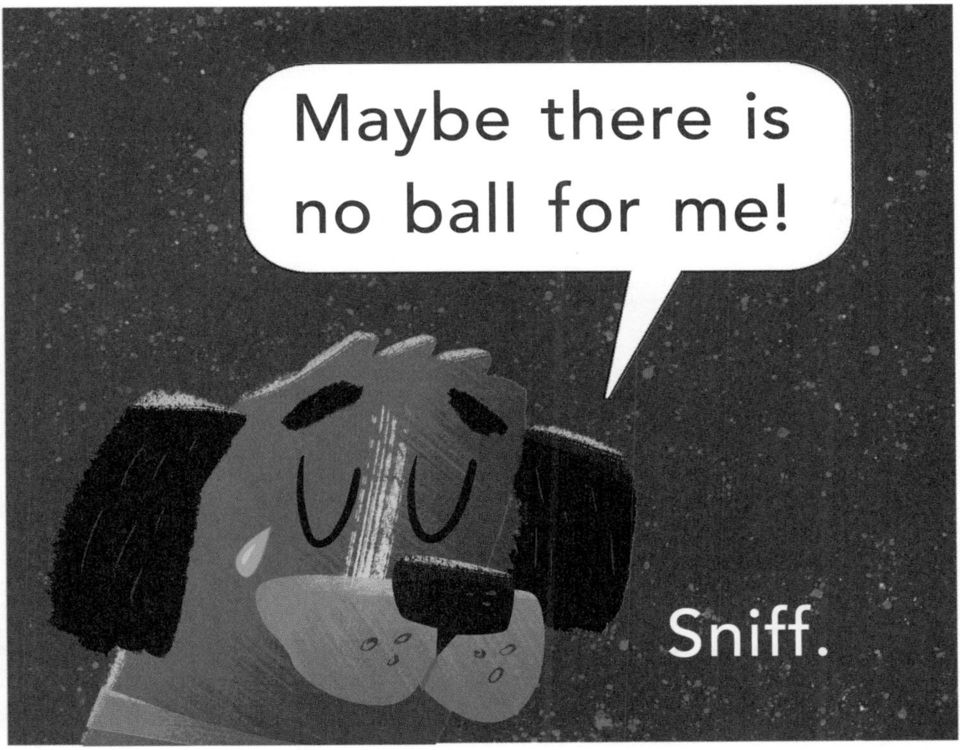
Maybe there is
no ball for me!
Sniff.

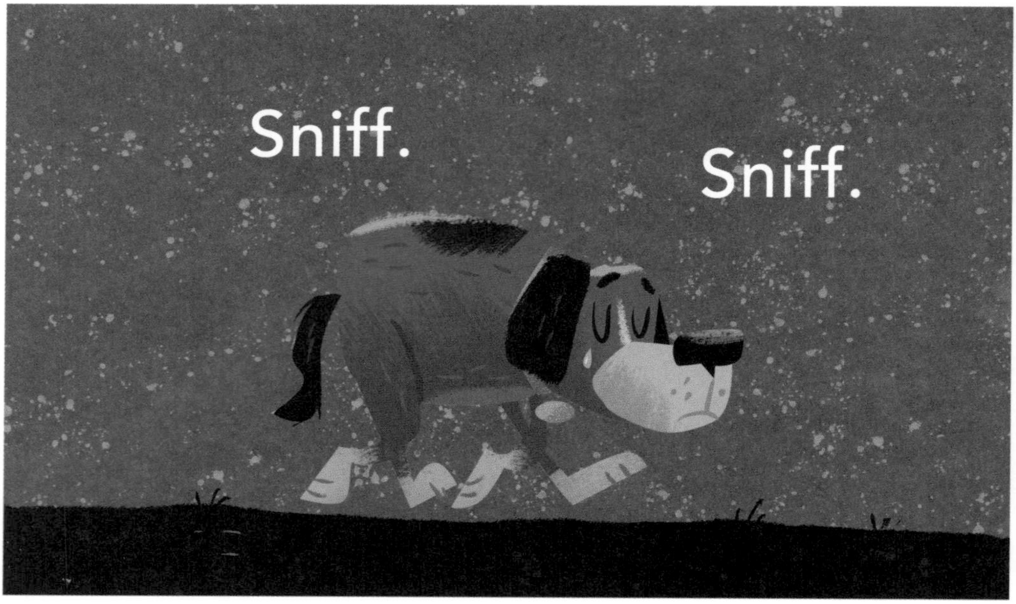
Sniff.
Sniff.

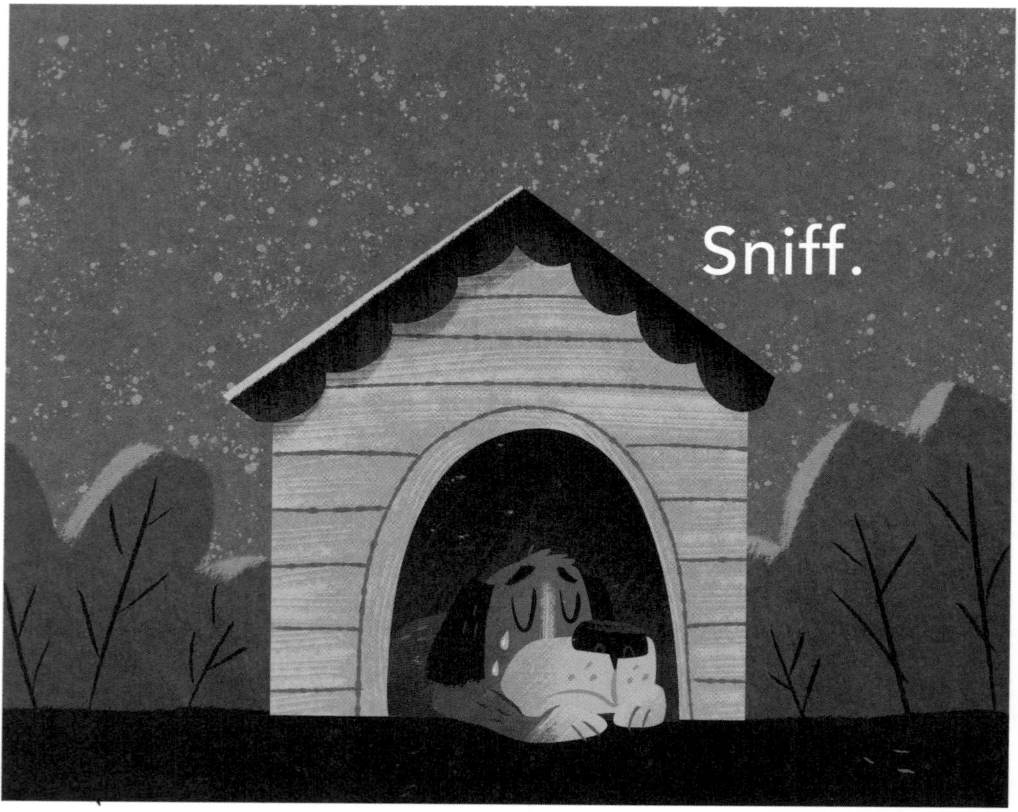
Sniff.

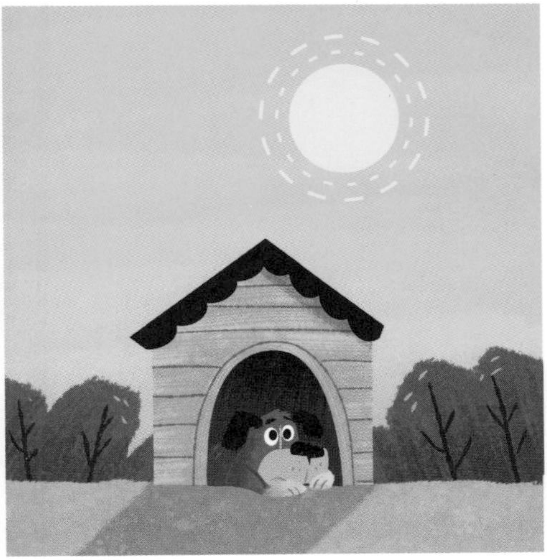

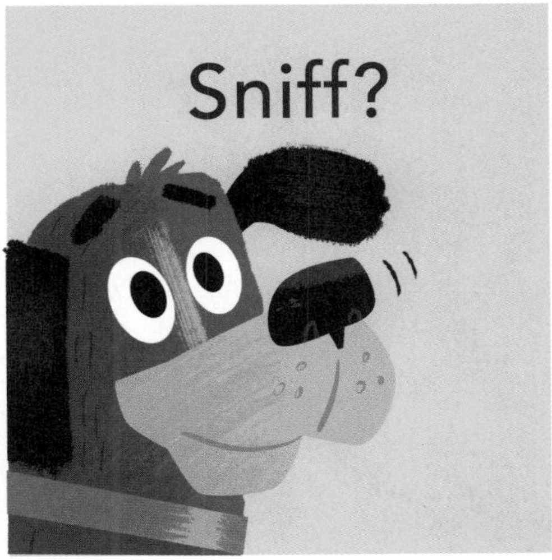
Sniff?

Sniff sniff sniff sniff sniff!

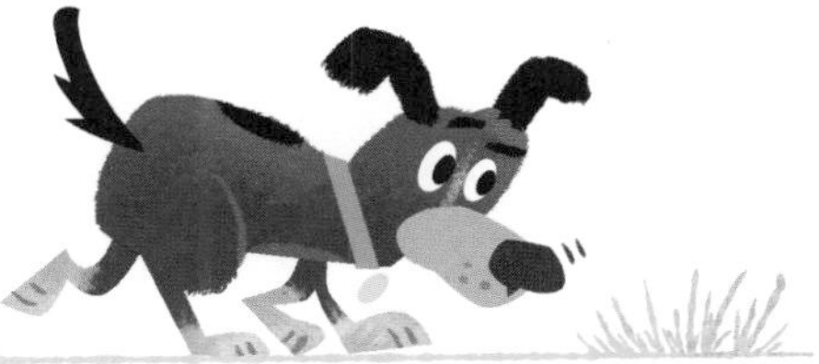

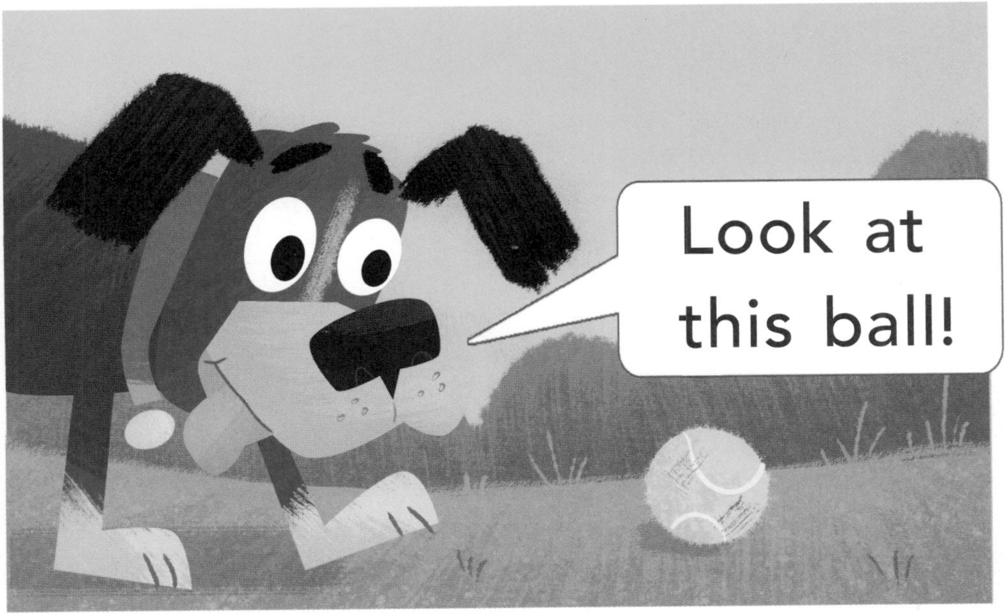
Look at this ball!

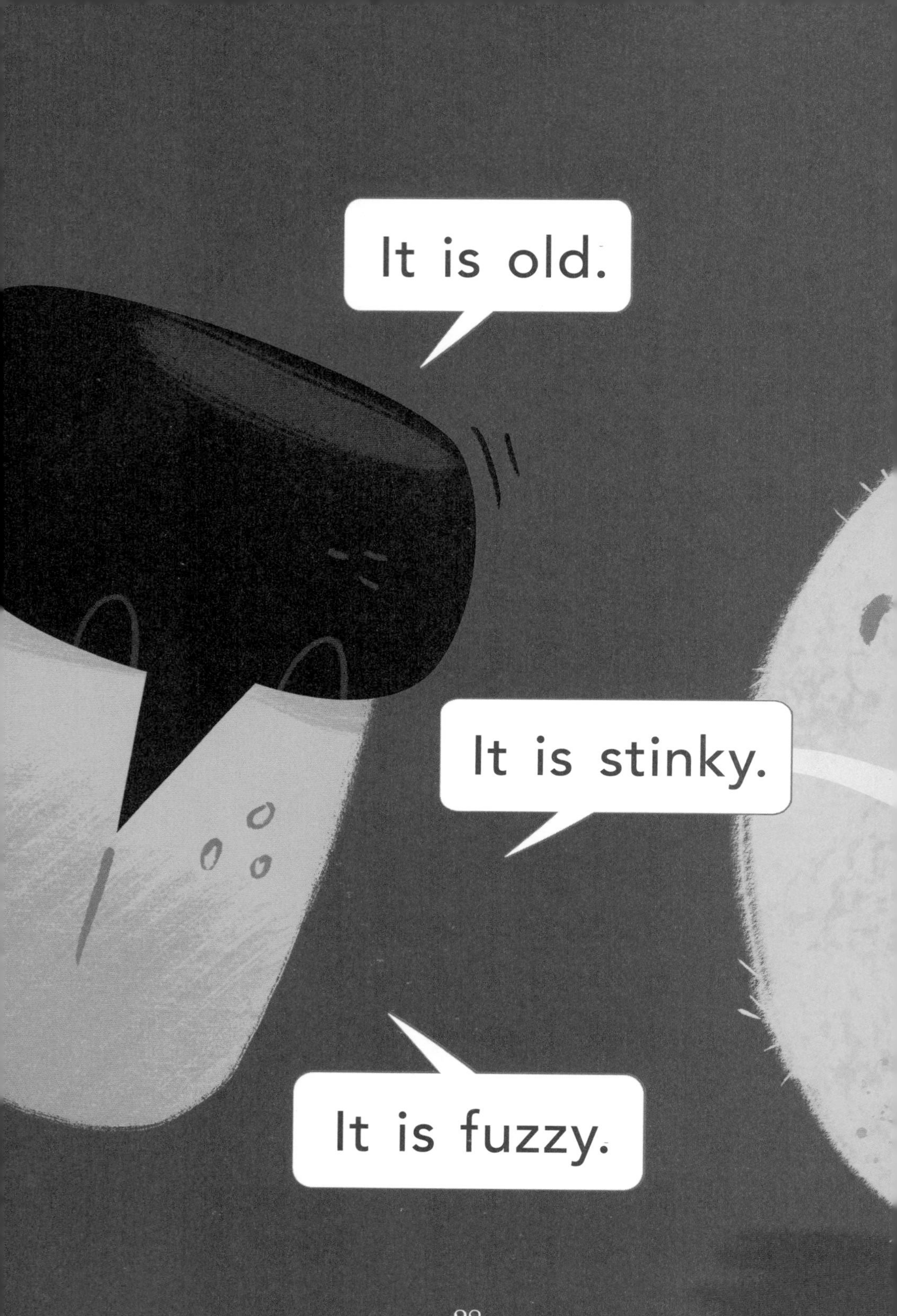
It is old.
It is stinky.
It is fuzzy.

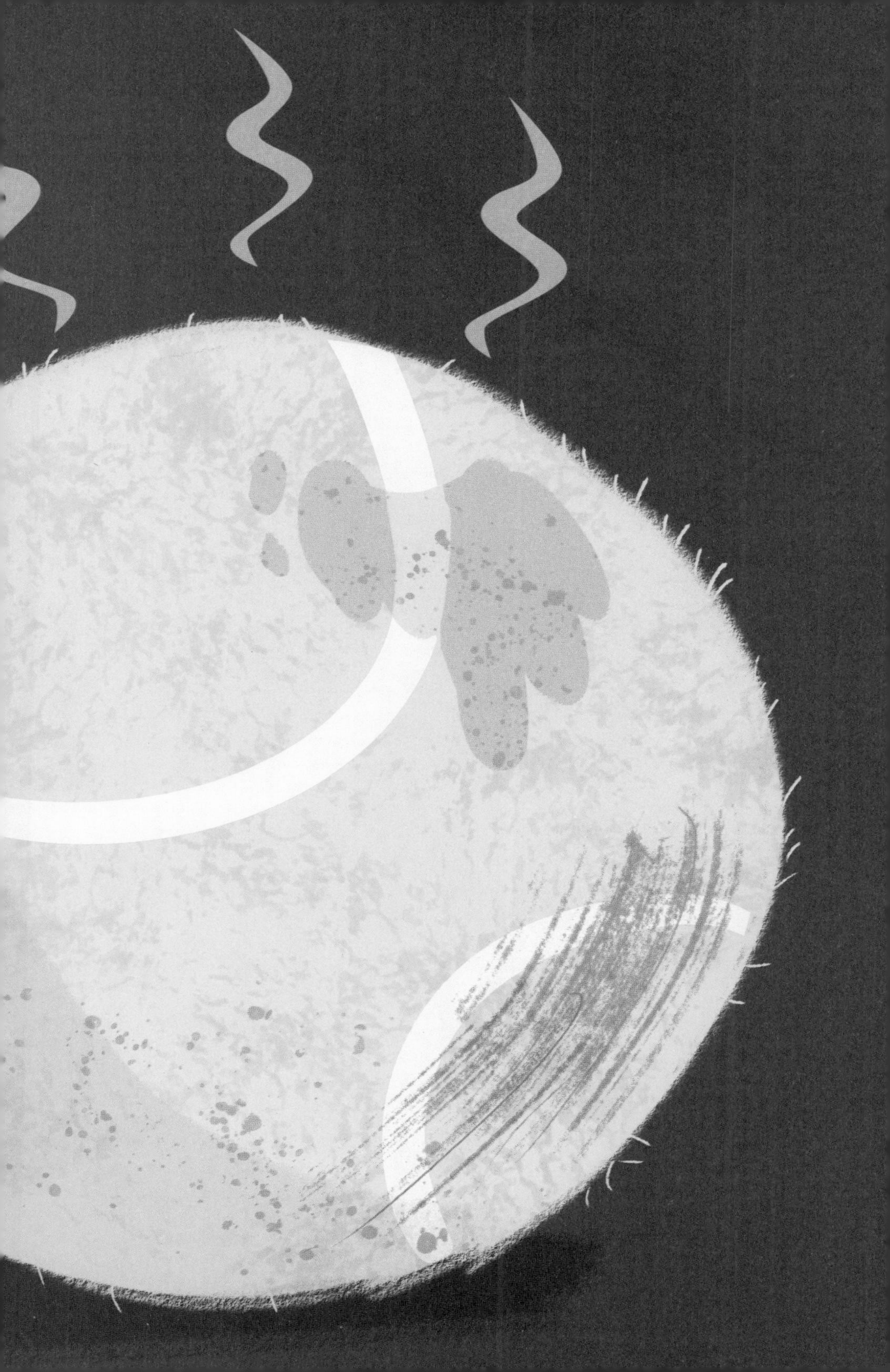

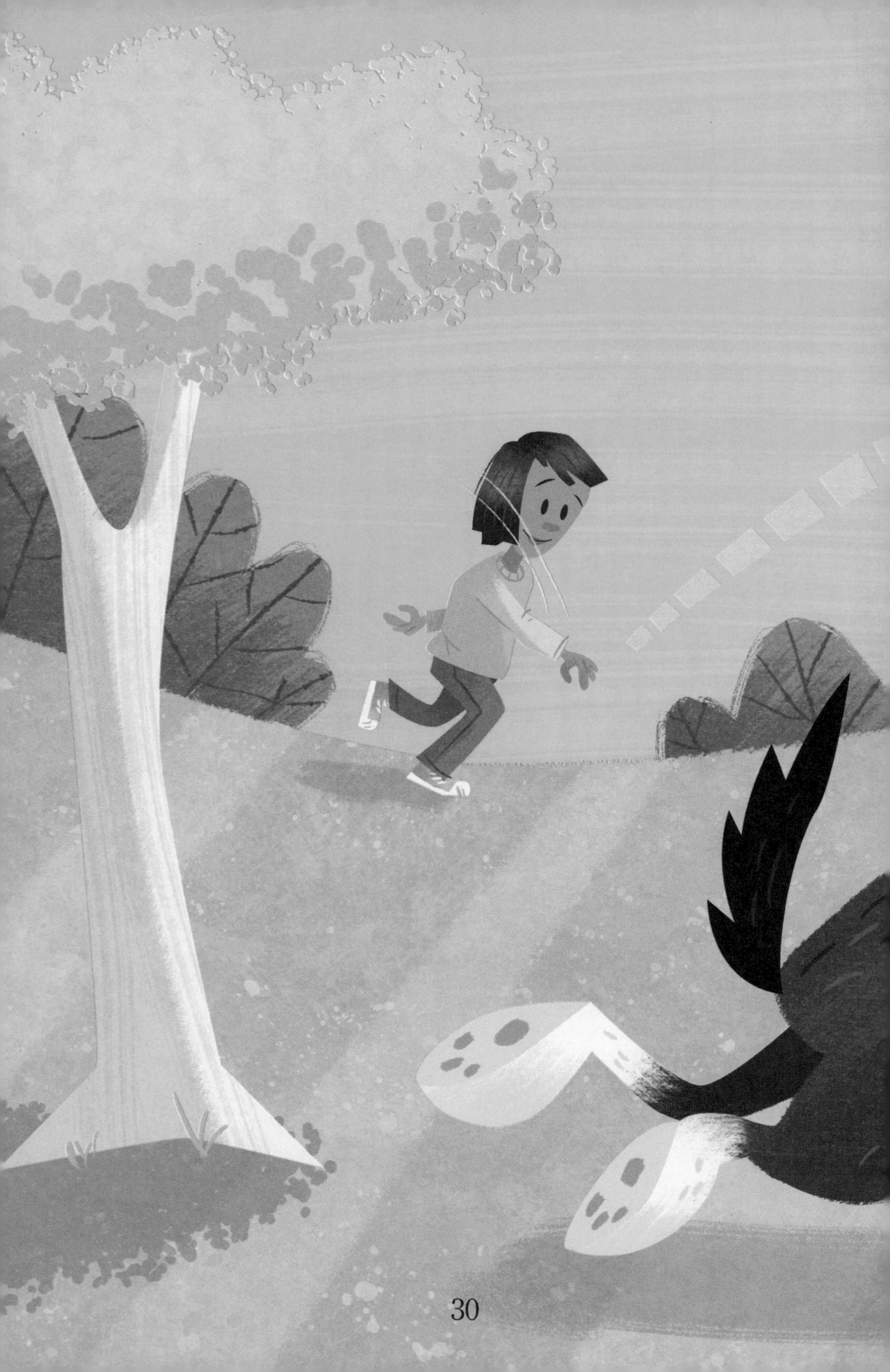

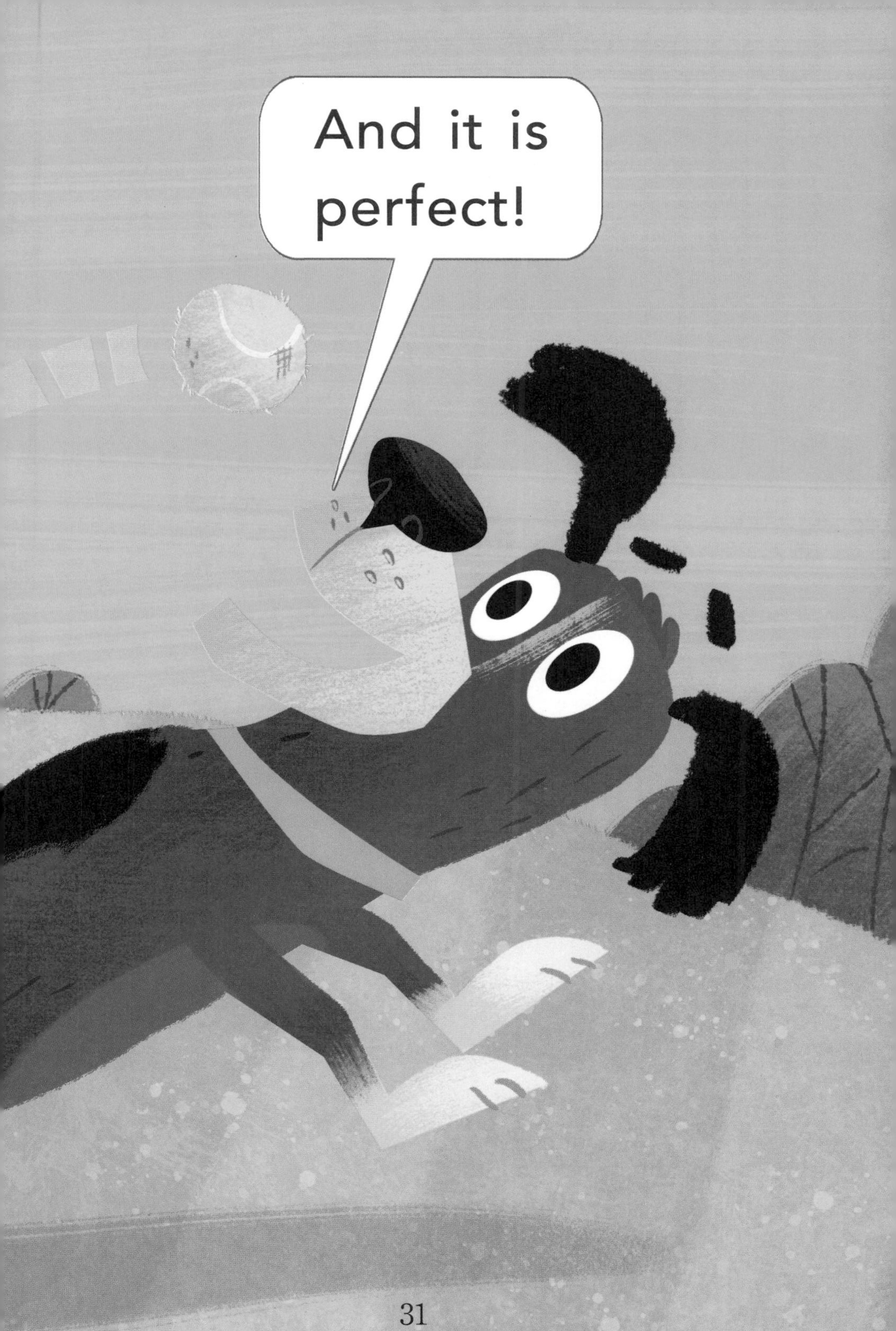
And it is perfect!